I0670584

A Ruined Wife

The seductions, submissions, and sexual encounters of ordinary housewives

Andrea's Story
Part III

Husband's Tramp

by **Mrs. Jennifer Nite**

FOR ADULTS ONLY

ISBN 978-0-9835225-2-2

The names of the participants of the encounters described in this book have all been changed to protect their identities and to respect their privacy.

Anyone wishing to contact the publisher can at provocativepublishers@gmail.com. You are also invited to contact the author at jennifernite@gmail.com. Comments and opinions are always appreciated.

About This Edition

This is a revised edition of the wildly popular eBook available on Kindle. You may ask if the revisions are worth purchasing the paperback. Good question.

The front and back cover photos have changed. (Yes, boys, the lady is a married friend of mine). There are also many grammatical fixes. Finally, there are substantive changes throughout the book which provide more detail in certain areas of the story. Parts II and III in particular have much more detail. The chapters have also been revised, for a total of 40 chapters through the end of Part III. All told, the three parts total well over 500 pages.

That all being said, I usually use eBooks on my iPhone just to pass tedious down time, such as when I'm trapped in an airport waiting hours for a flight. Personally, I am the kind of person who has to own a copy of a book if it's in print. There is just nothing like holding a hard copy of a book in your hands. It also makes it easier for your spouse to innocently "find" the story lying around the house!

– Jennifer

Introduction

The ordinary.

That's the life of most people. We get up in the morning, we go through the work day waiting for it to end, and we come home to take care of our children and husbands. And then we go to bed, roll over, and ... it starts all over again. Day after day. Year after year. The drudgery of married life. I know . . . I've experienced it myself for 16 years.

But sex is not ordinary. Sex is extraordinary. But inevitably sex leaves the marriage after a period of years. And what do you do then? Suffer through life?

This is a series that explores that question from the perspective of several married women, with loving husbands and often with young children. Some are younger ladies, and some are older.

The results are the same -- a sexual awakening that changes their lives. They become ruined to the ordinary sexually-empty drudgery of the monogamous marriage. And their husbands become accepting and often participating cuckolds (archaically known as wittols).

Is it a moral issue? I can't answer that question. It used to be that sexual awareness was a topic explored by men, and often (but not always) shunned by women.

The men's stag films and the pulp fiction novels of the 50s and 60s changed dramatically with the advent of the Internet. Morals widened, sexual freedom has expanded, and pornography is secretly available to everyone virtually for free. And women are now active consumers. MILF is now a universally known word. Being seen as a beautiful MILF is remarkably the goal of many wives and mothers throughout the United States and, indeed, the world.

The transformation of our society is what led to these stories. I do not pass judgment on these ladies or their husbands. I understand what a little on the side can do for one's outlook on life.

The stories speak almost exclusively of the sexual encounters of ordinary housewives and mothers, women I would consider to be genuine ladies. These are the women who are your next-door neighbor, the gorgeous wife you see at the PTO meeting, that tremendously hot girl you see at the office every day.

The places in these stories are everywhere, from their homes to their offices and everywhere in between.

Be warned! The tales of these married women are not for the lighthearted. Unlike most books in this genre, these books are not romance novels and they are not stories of lovemaking.

They are likewise not a collection of short stories that you have to read 10 pages to get to what you want, just to find that it's little or nothing. These are hard core, very explicit stories that get right to the point in great detail. They are XXX, no question about it. The wives present in graphic detail and usually from their perspective the circumstances that led to their seduction . . . blow by blow, so to speak.

It's mainstream encounters, from the single seduction -- often forced for the first time – to threesomes and even the occasional gang action. Their partners are white, black, and everyone else. But there are no water sports, no bondage, no whips and chains, no beating of people, no animals, no children, no incest, and no weird sexual acts. If you need any of that sort of thing, then you will need to go elsewhere.

You should also avoid these books if you are easily offended by filthy, sordid talk, because that is the essence of the seductions. So be careful! These books are so hot you'll burn yourself.

A word of warning before you continue. We won't patronize you, because we trust that you are all mature, consenting adults. But we caution you to seriously consider the ramifications before embarking on the lifestyle presented in this series. Provocative Publishers believes in the importance and value of family relationships.

Jealously and insecurity are the scourge of families. If you are considering an open-marriage kind of lifestyle, please do everything possible to preserve your family. You have a choice. Some people, like we will see with Andrea, didn't have a choice. The exhilaration of the lifestyle was forced upon her, after which she couldn't turn back!

So, if you want to hear the details of the seductions of beautiful housewives and the endless sex they have come to need -- how each has become ruined to the ordinary drudgery of married life -- then read on. You will not be disappointed with these tales of infidelity!

We invite you to read the whole series. They each tell a different story from a different perspective!

Who knows. Maybe some film producer would like to adapt these stories to the screen. There certainly aren't any good XXX films out there that present these kinds of stories versus all of that mindless stupid porn in the world. If you're an interested adult film producer, give us a shout.

That all being said, let's finish my friend Andrea's story. In the next book, we'll hear from Helen, a 44 year old lady married to a doctor who cheats on her. Needless to say, those tables get turned!

My Story Continues!

To remind you of who I am, my name is Andrea, and I have become a nymphomaniac cock whore. This my continuing story of how some bastards introduced me to this lifestyle.

If you haven't read the first two parts, *Reluctant Tramp* and *Seduced Tramp*, you really need to. It's the only way you can understand how I came to this point in my life. And, I would add, they are great reads.

I'm a 36 year old pretty brunette housewife and mother, and I look good - if I say so myself! You couldn't tell that I have two children. My husband's name is Mark. We've been married for 11 years. Mark had been the only man I'd ever been with until Bill got his prick into me.

I'd been a good girl after that fateful day, and I had another baby girl with my husband since that time. I took a whole year off from cheating after that 24-hour period of whoring. In *Seduced Tramp*, you heard how my boss got me into a whorish lifestyle after I came back to work from my maternity leave.

You will recall that Mark just wasn't satisfying me, and I had to use dildos to satisfy myself. My horniness started to become increasingly overwhelming, especially after strange men constantly came into the bank and talked to me.

Each day I fought the horny urges, trying to control the uncontrollable. As hard as I tried to be good, it was a bad situation that was bound to get worse. I had to succumb to my urges, and I did.

Now to the rest of my story . . . let me tell you how my husband has became an active participant in my new lifestyle.

OUR lifestyle!

Chapter 29

We left off after my re-awakening to my sexual needs. I had finally been able to introduce my husband to the idea of an open marriage. In fact, I was lucky enough to help him see that it was HIS need and desire – and his idea – to see me fuck other men!

It was a tremendous day of constant fucking with several men, culminating in that wonderful night of my husband's awakening. I knew the next day was important. Very important. My problems were close to being solved.

The only issue I faced was how to implement it before Mark changed his mind. I knew I had to act quick. But I was nervous. Very nervous.

Mark and I laid in bed together all morning, holding each other and fucking. I didn't bring up other men, though, because I wanted him to do that. Maybe he was tired and didn't mean it. I didn't want to appear to eager about the idea, so I just waited for the opportunity to discuss it further with him. Let me tell you, it was hard for me to wait to see how it would go.

Mark eventually looked at me and asked if I remembered discussing sex and fantasies. When I said that I had, he told me that it was up to me and that he wasn't going to pressure me if I wanted to do a threesome with him.

Not wanting to let this golden chance pass, I gave him my terms.

I told Mark that I loved him dearly, and that I would do anything to please him. But my marriage was most important, and I wouldn't do anything to jeopardize it.

Mark agreed with me.

I went on to say that I would put out to other men for him, but that he had to be submissive so we didn't scare them away.

Mark agreed again, but he added another term.

"Our marriage is also the most important thing to me," he said, " so we have to agree that we won' have sex with anyone else until the other knows about it and is there . . . no matter how much you like it."

Mark was afraid of losing me, which I completely understood. I never wanted to cheat on him in the first place. I just had to relieve the horny ache that Bill planted in me. I readily agreed. It was a simple solution to satisfy my dark desires.

There was excitement in the bedroom as we talked about it more. I think we fucked at least two more times since the conversation started.

We agreed that we would try a trial run. We set about making a plan. We decided that the following weekend we would go to a bar and find a lucky stud to enjoy me. I told him that I would fuck any man he picked out for me. If everything went alright, the next time he would let me fuck any man I chose.

I told Mark that I was concerned about how the evening would develop. We would be with a total stranger, not knowing a thing about him. What boundaries would we draw?

We agreed that we would let the man do and say whatever he wanted, and that we would submit to his desires as long as they didn't cross into the bizarre.

What if he wanted to bareback me? Would be that ok?

Mark said he loved sex without a condom, but he was worried He said he preferred it if the man had a condom, but should we stop it if he didn't? We discussed that issue a lot. It is a serious decision that has to be made.

Mark also asked if I was on the pill. I was afraid to admit that I was, because he always thought that I wasn't. I told him I would go to my OBGYN on Monday.

We talked about backing out once the man was with us. To avoid any potential problems, we agreed that once it was started, it was started – unless the guy was some kind of weirdo. In that case either of us could end it then and there by using the magic word. {Sorry, the magic word is our secret!}

But for the sex component, we agreed there would be no limits as long as the sex was mainstream. I would take anything the man could give me, no matter how big his cock turned out to be, and Mark would not say anything negative or interfere. But no whips, ropes, chains, . . .

We also agreed it would be a true threesome to the extent it could be. Mark could participate to his heart's content.

"What about talk?" I asked. "What if he says filthy things about me?"

"I thought you liked it from what I could tell," Mark responded.

"Well, it was kind of exciting," I said.

So we agreed that any of us could say anything we wanted, no matter how vile or filthy. The talk would be just that - talk. It would be no reflection of how we truly felt, and it would be no reflection on the love we felt for each other.

What a set up!

Mark asked about something else. It took me by surprise, because I loved it. But I wasn't thinking and forgot that Mark thought I was an ass virgin.

"What if he wants to fuck you in the ass?" Mark asked.

I paused for a moment. How does one answer that question when yes, they really want to get ass fuck. Put it back on him.

"Well, I don't know," I responded. "What do you think we should do if he wants sex from behind?"

I couldn't believe it. Mark gave a dream come true answer.

"Well, Andrea," he said, "if you want to take other men like a slut, how can you say no? Everyone does it nowadays."

Ah, Mark wanted me to ass fuck! But he always thought I would say no! Well, he was right. I would have said no.

"Ok," I said, "let's see how it goes. You know how I am about anal sex."

I couldn't believe the words that were coming out of my mouth. It sure would be interesting if the lucky stud wanted to pop my ass!

I was a wreck the whole week. It was hard to think straight. But I did make sure Mark kept his interest in our arrangement. We talked about it every night, usually ending with a hot fuck.

Jack desperately tried to rekindle his lost opportunity to satisfy the desires he knew I had. But I came to hate the man. I wouldn't let him near me.

I also felt a deep sense of redemption. I had a deal with my wonderful husband that I firmly believed would strengthen our marriage and solve our horny needs to boot. There was no need to cheat on the man I loved any more. I honestly believed it, and I believe it to this day.

With bated anticipation, I pushed myself through the work week, getting more horny as each day went by.

It got worse as Mark and I constantly discussed it during the week. We talked about how I would dress. I didn't have any clothes that would fit that need, so Mark and I went out one evening and picked up a wonderfully sexy dress that would surely do the trick.

It was a slinky, sleeveless, short red dress that tightly hugged my body. It was very low-cut with an open back, so we also decided that I would skip the bra to better tease the lucky stud we intended to land.

Stockings and panties of any kind were out of the question. That night I would go bear legs with open-toed high heels. Let the men enjoy my flaming red nails!

And make-up. Tonight I put on a glossy red lipstick. I also wore very dark eye shadow and mascara. An enticing perfume topped it all off.

There was no question about it. I would certainly look like a horny married lady starving for hard cock.

Chapter 30

Saturday night finally came.

We took the kids to their grandparents for the night, and then went home to get ready. It took me a while to get my makeup on in a whorish, yet tasteful way. My trademark red nails and lipstick, dark eye shadow, and very enticing perfume.

I got dressed up in my new red fuck outfit, putting on the sexiest heels that I owned. An ankle bracelet completed the ensemble to show off my shapely legs. Mark and I knew that we wanted someone who would appreciate fucking a horny married woman – a MILF cougar – so I also made sure to wear my wedding rings.

The stage was set. Now, where to go?

Mark and I had discussed it during the week, but we never made a final decision. Needless to say, the Roundup bar was out of the question because of my escapades their in the past, so I never mentioned it. Besides, I didn't really want a sleazy bar. We needed a nice night club.

Mark said he knew of a little dance club in a neighboring town, so we decided to head there. It was very convenient that there was a little strip motel across the street.

There was an absolute electrical excitement in the air as we set out to fulfill my husband's lusty desires, going out looking to get his wife laid by a strange man.

Mark rubbed my thighs during the entire trip, occasionally running his hand between my legs. I'm sure he could tell that I was getting wet.

I couldn't stand it. I spread my legs and started fingering myself as he glanced over while he drove. I rubbed his crotch with my other hand, getting his cock hard.

We talked more about what was going to happen as I fingered my pussy. We were both exciting ourselves more with the conversation, and in no time we had the conversation down to a vile level.

"Oh, Mark, what if his cock is just too big?" I asked.

"Sweetheart, I know you can handle any cock out there," he responded in an actual loving way.

"Will you stuff your cock in my mouth when he opens me up?" I asked.

My husband was thrilled at the prospect, exhilarated like I had never seen him before.

"Just don't bite me when he slams his cock into you!" he said.

We both laughed. It helped to break the tense air.

I think we were both nervously excited beyond belief when we finally arrived at he club. As we walked in, I could notice all of the male eyes turning to watch me as I strolled in.

It was a fairly crowded place, so I think we were quite lucky when we found a table in the corner. We sat down and talked about how we would meet people. Our plan was for Mark to leave for drinks.

Sure enough, Mark no sooner left and I was approached by the first stud sniffing out something to fuck. It was blatantly obvious that he was looking for a piece of ass by the way he tried to cling onto me while throwing out the stupid one liners.

I was pleased when Mark came back and asked if he could help the man. The asshole made a rude remark to Mark. I was afraid it was going to start a fight, but the dickhead backed off and went away.

Mark then made it clear to me that he had no intention of letting that kind of asshole fuck me. It was a statement I had to agree with given my experiences with Jack.

For some reason, you could never get rid of the assholes. They barged into your life demanding sex whenever they wanted it. I knew that was something I definitely wanted to avoid in the future.

We went through about twenty men this way, letting them come up to talk to me, and to show what assholes they were at the same time. We laughed when we came to the conclusion that my outfit had to be an asshole magnet.

We were starting to get discouraged that we weren't going to find a nice guy who would appreciate married ass. Eventually, though, our luck turned when we met Travis.

Mark and I were sitting at the table talking, when Travis came up and introduced himself. He was kind of geeky looking, no doubt about it. But he was very polite and complimenting. I'd say he was about 25 years old, and a good 6' tall.

Travis walked up to us and said sheepishly that he couldn't help but notice us. He said we looked like a happy couple. He asked if he might join us for a drink. Mark invited him to sit down.

We sat and talked for a while, joking about all of the bullshit that goes on in the world. He was an incredibly suave and assertive young man, not afraid to share his opinions. He was also avoiding being a lech, complimenting me on my looks without staring.

Travis finally asked Mark if he could dance with me, actually asking permission. It was then that I knew we found a slick stud in disguise. I mean, my God. Who would ask a man if he could dance with his wife unless he wanted to fuck her?!?

Travis and I danced a fast number, and when it was over Travis asked if I wanted to continue dancing. I could hear a slow number beginning, so I told him that I would love to. He took me in his arms, and we danced closely for a few minutes. I was surprised as he started to rub his hand over my back, politely but with enough daring to see if it was welcome. I didn't say a word. I only rubbed his back to indicate that his attention was welcome.

Travis and I stayed out on the dance floor longer, and I could notice my husband watching from a distance. Travis got the message, and he led me back to the table.

We engaged in some mindless small talk for a bit longer. Finally, Mark asked me to dance. He left some money on the table and asked Travis to buy us another round. It was a clear signal to Travis that he didn't have to leave.

When Mark and I were out on the dance floor, we danced closely. He whispered in my ear.

"Do you like him?" he asked me.

"Yes, he's nice," I said, "but I agreed you could pick anybody you wanted and I would fuck him."

"I know sweetheart," he said, "but it's important to me that you like him too."

God, how I loved this man! He was the first man in all of my adventures who cared what I wanted.

"He's a nice young boy," I responded, "I'll fuck him if you want me to."

Mark didn't say a word. He just kissed me until the song was over, and then we headed back to the table.

As soon as I got back, Travis asked me to dance again. Why not, I said.

Travis and I danced two fast songs, and then the slow music started again. He took me in his strong hands and held me tight. I rested my head next to his. After seeing me kiss Mark on the dance floor, I think Travis knew where this was heading.

The young stud held me close, and our bodies writhed together to the music. He eventually started moving his hands down from my back, gently rubbing as he made his way to my ass. I felt so decadently fantastic to be rubbed in public by this stranger while my husband approvingly watched!

When the slow numbers stopped, we went back to the table. Travis got up to go to the men's room, which gave me the opportunity to discuss the matter further with Mark.

There was no doubt about it. We both liked Travis, and we decided that we would find a way to ask him to a motel for an evening of sex.

Travis apparently had the same idea. He returned to the table and moved his glass where he could sit a lot closer to me.

I then put on more lipstick as my signal that this my vote for a stud.

I made a point of rubbing my hands through my hair, bending over so Travis could see my big tits in all their glory. I even bent over to get something out of my purse, giving him a clear view of the prize.

Travis was definitely getting excited, which caused him to bring his hand over to my leg. He rubbed it softly, laughing with me and my husband. I made sure not to say a word.

Travis got more bold as the evening wore on, running his hands up by the hem of my short dress. In a flash his hand went under.

As an instinctive reaction. I spread my legs slightly so he could feel me up. He was certainly delighted to find that I had no panties on, running his fingers through my cunt lips and into my pussy.

Mark knew what he was doing, but he didn't want to scare Travis off. He commented nonchalantly.

"My wife's really a beautiful woman, isn't she Travis?"

"She is remarkable," Travis responded.

Mark then leaned over to kiss me, running his tongue into my mouth. As he did so, I reached over and rubbed Travis's crotch.

I was enchanted by the bulge I felt, a hard-on that had to signify a rather large cock. How lucky!

After we felt each other up for about ten minutes, Travis again asked me to dance to a slow number. I readily accepted.

When we were finally out on the floor, Travis took me tightly into his arms. He hands immediately started feeling my ass, grinding his hard-on into my cunt as we danced around the floor.

I wasn't surprised when we finally looked into each other eyes, our lips locking in what would soon be a wonderful night. Travis just took me, driving his hand up my dress and between my legs, openly copping a feel of my naked pussy.

I could feel his hot breath against my neck as he moved closer. He whispered in my ear as he felt me up.

"I'd love to stroke my cock off right here," he said as he pushed his fingers into my went cunt. I felt so hot and beautiful as he said it.

I squeezed Travis hard as he said those words, turning my head to lick his ear.

"You'd love to suck my big cock, wouldn't you," he asked.

"Mmmmm . . . ," I responded.

"What about your husband?" he eventually asked.

"Mark loves to see me fuck other men," I told him.

"Goddamn," Travis said, "he can watch me pound you all night long!"

Travis saw Mark watch us on the dance floor, so he knew my husband was in on this. Mark kissed me when we got back, and that no doubt sealed the deal.

I got up to go to the ladies room, to give the men a chance to talk. According to Mark, Travis remarked that I was incredibly sexy, and that Mark was a lucky guy to have such a wife.

Mark agreed with him, telling him that he wouldn't believe I was a hot number in the sack.

He told me that Travis looked at me with a wide grin.

"I'd sure love to find out," he said.

"I'm sure you would!" Mark responded.

Mark told me that Travis then got bolder, and quite frank.

"I told her I wanted to fuck her," he admitted to Mark.

"What did she say?" Mark responded.

"She said I could fuck her all night long if I let you watch."

By this time, I was almost back at the table. I barely heard the words "let you watch", and I knew our mission was accomplished.

When I got back, I inserted myself between the two men. Both men soon had their hands up my dress, feeling up my cunt. I could feel both their hands, often time fighting to see who could get their fingers into me! What an exciting feeling!

The secret was definitely out then, as both hands worked out some kind of sharing arrangement to get their fingers into my pussy. In no time, I was publicly taking long kisses from both men.

Enough of this foreplay, I decided.

I looked at Mark and told him that we should get going. He agreed.

I then looked at Travis and asked the simplest question to seal the deal.

"So, Travis, how would you and Mark like to screw me tonight?"

"I'd love to join you two," he responded with a wide grin.

We all got up and walked out to the parking lot. We showed Travis the car we were driving. Travis agreed to follow us to the motel across the street.

I was feeling quite randy on the short ride to the motel. As close as it was, it still took was too long. I needed cock. And I need it NOW!

I wanted to show Mark that he made the right decision as we drove through the motel's parking lot. I hiked up my dress to reveal my legs. Mark smiled as I spread my legs and slowly ran my fingers through my hairy bush, enticing him about Travis as he parked.

"You sure you want that stranger to stick his hard cock in me?" I teased.

Mark was quick to respond.

"I really do Andrea," he said, "I've always wanted to see another man enjoy you."

I stuck my fingers into my pussy, drawing out the slick cunt juice and rubbing it on my bush.

"I think he's really going to enjoy this," I whispered.

"Damn, Andrea, I never imagined you could be so fucking hot!" Mark exclaimed.

I brought my fingers to his mouth and let him lick the cunt juice off from them. I then reached over and rubbed the raging hard-on in his pants.

"I'm hot for you," I reassured him, "I want to have a hot marriage where I fulfill your every fantasy!"

Mark smiled, loving every word he was hearing. I wanted him to love it some more. So I bent over and kissed his stiff cock through his pants.

"Damn!" he said, "God I love you!"

"I love you too," I whispered back.

I was the happiest woman alive.

Chapter 31

Mark rented a sleazy motel room while Travis and I went down the road a few miles to buy some beer at a convenience store. It was a lot like the one Bill, Sam and Pete screwed me in.

I was feeling a little tipsy, so I agreed to go with Travis when he asked me to join him. Mark was somewhat drunk himself, so he didn't object.

"Have fun," he said, "but hurry back."

It probably wasn't the smartest decision we made, but thankfully it worked out.

I rubbed Travis' crotch as he drove down the road. Like Mark, Travis also had a raging hard-on. I stroked his cock through his pants the whole way. We french kissed once we got to the convenience store while he felt up my dripping cunt.

Travis ran in to the store and was out in a flash. This man was motivated, I thought! I was incredibly horny. As soon as Travis was back in the car, I continued rubbing his crotch as he fondled my thighs.

Travis couldn't wait any more. He brought his hand up from my leg and placed it on the back of my neck. He pulled me down.

I had never given a man a blowjob in the car. But I couldn't wait any longer either. I let Travis guide my head down. I bent over and unzipped his pants.

I reached into his trousers and freed the stiff prick as Travis stroked my hair. I was delighted to pull out a stiff 10" cock. Travis didn't lie to me on the dance floor. He did have a big cock for me to suck.

I moaned as I saw the fuck stick. I grabbed it and started jerking it furiously.

"You wanna suck my hard cock, sweetheart?" he asked me.

I didn't need much encouragement. I needed to feel a cock in my mouth right then and there. I smiled and him and went down, slipping Travis' big cock into my watering mouth.

"Damn!" Travis said, "you are so fucking hot Andrea!"

His words sent me over the edge. Yes, I was hot. I was so hot, in fact, that I took his entire shaft down my throat in an instant.

Travis started moaning as I face fucked his cock, running his fingers through my hair.

"Damn Andrea, you really know how to suck cock!" he moaned.

If he only knew!

As I sucked him off, Travis reached into my dress and started to feel up my tits. It made me suck him harder and harder. I withdrew completely every few seconds to give his shaft a furious hand job.

It didn't take long. By the time the short ride was over, I drew cum from the young stud. What an inexperienced boy, I thought!

Travis had a copious load. He filled my mouth in no time. I didn't want to swallow yet, so some dribbled out onto my chin so he could see it. Cum on a woman's face seems to be the single biggest turn on for men – well, except seeing a double penetration in action!

Once the fuck stick was drained, I looked Travis straight in the eye and swirled his cum in my open mouth, rubbing the rest around my chin.

"I love cum," I said with a grin.

"Oh fuck . . ." he said in response to the decadent show.

I swallowed with a big gulp, and then I used my fingers to gather up the cum on my chin. Cum webs formed between my fingers, and I licked them clean.

"God, I really love cum Travis," I whispered in his ear, leaning over and kissing his neck.

I rested my head on Travis' lap all the way home, playing with his limp cock. He reached over and felt up by tits as he drove, causing his cock to start to harden again. I was starting to give him a gentle hand job as he rounded the corner to the hotel and parked.

God, I was one happy woman!

Chapter 32

Once we arrived back at the motel, Travis zipped his pants up. I jumped out of the car and headed for the room, Travis close on my tail.

As soon as we walked into the motel room, Mark came up to me and put his arm around my waist. He kissed me and then gave me a grin.

"Do I taste cum in your mouth," he whispered in my ear.

"He asked me to suck him off," I whispered back with a grin, "and I didn't want to be impolite!"

Mark smiled, obviously loving the fact that I sucked this stud off in the car. He then looked at Travis and smiled, going out into the hall to get some ice.

Travis didn't waste any time taking me in his arms and kissing me while Mark slipped out, his pecker forming a noticeable hard-on that he began to grind into my snatch.

When Mark came back, he handed Travis a beer and asked him to pick out some music that he had on his iPhone.

Mark then sat in the chair, and I went and sat on his lap.

Travis picked out some light jazz and played it on the phone. He then sat on the bed and watched as Mark and I kissed. Mark ran his hands up my dress to expose my bare legs for our new friend.

As soon as Mark started to work his hand between my legs, I made sure to spread them for Travis. I wanted him to see Mark run his fingers through my thick hairy bush.

Travis was obviously quite comfortable with the situation, sitting on the bed and making innocuous comments as he watched us.

"Andrea, you're such an incredibly beautiful lady," he said.

I looked at him and smiled as I bit my lips, showing thanks for the compliment.

Eventually, Travis wanted his share. He asked if he could help.

Without uttering a word, I slipped off from Mark's lap and onto the floor. I crawled over to Travis on my hands and knees like a horny slut looking for cock. I moved in between his spread legs, clearly a cougar in heat.

I unzipped Travis' pants and reached in. I then pulled out his stiff 10" prick for Mark to see. This was new to Mark, and as far as he was concerned, this was all new to me.

I wanted to go slow and act kind of innocent. I certainly did not want to exhibit myself as the whore that was so thoroughly trained by Bill and Al. Besides, I had to make sure Mark got into this.

I looked back at Mark as I stroked Travis's thick prick.

"God, Mark," I said, "his cock is so thick."

Mark smiled at me.

"Go for it, Andrea, enjoy yourself," he responded, "give the man some more head."

"Some more head?" I said with a devilish grin.

"Yes, baby, some more head," he responded with a laugh.

That was all I needed to hear. I turned back and looked up at Travis.

"Would you like me to give you some more head Travis?"

Travis was quick in his response.

"I'd love to feel more of that hot mouth of yours sweetheart."

I slipped the cock head into my mouth and snapped my lips shut on it. I slowly started stroking it with my mouth as the two men enjoyed my performance. I then sucked the massive cock head for a few minutes. I moved on to lick up and down on the hard shaft.

I reached down and started to rub Travis's ball sac with my nails as I licked. I then brought my head around to start bobbing on the throbbing fuck stick. It was definitely good head for Travis. He leaned his head back on he cushion and started to let out a low moan.

I sucked Travis's cock like this for a few minutes, stopping every now and again to lick his balls. It was now time for the master move.

I took the shaft and held it straight in the air. In a flash my mouth was on it, and I slowly worked the fucker into my mouth. Travis went nuts.

"Ohhhhh fuck," he said as he started to rub my hair. I reached around him so I could get leverage to throat him.

Travis lifted his head to watch me swallow his dick, looking over to Mark to make a comment.

"Man, can your wife suck cock," Travis said. Mark was quick to smile in agreement.

I eventually got he cock head lodged deep into my throat, which was my cue to start stroking it with my tongue.

Swirling my tongue against the soft underside of the shaft, I slowly withdrew the long cock from my mouth, only to immediately re-impale myself on the stick. I did this about five times, making Travis moaner louder and louder with each throat stroke.

On the fifth stroke I could feel something warm. I knew I had started to draw cum from the young stud again.

I pulled my mouth away from the cock head, leaving a long strong of thick pre-cum hanging from the head to my lower lip. After making sure that the men saw this, I stuck out my tongue and slowly collected the pre-cum, running it over my lips.

I looked up at Mark and started the remarks that I knew he would love.

"I want to feel his hot prick between my legs, Mark," I moaned to my husband. "Can I please fuck him?"

Without waiting for an answer, I looked up at Travis.

"If you cum in my mouth again, will you still be able to fuck me?" I asked. The stranger looked down and smiled.

"Nothing could keep me away from that pussy of yours, so go ahead and take another load down that pretty little throat of yours!"

That was all I needed to hear.

I took the shaft and drove it down my throat again. Pulling it out, I knew the throbbing fucker was ready to blow another wad. I locked my lips under the ridge of the cock head and jacked the shaft furiously. In no less than a minute, Travis started to unload in my mouth.

I knew it was incredibly important that this session satisfy Mark's darkest needs. I was determined to use this marriage-awakening encounter to fulfill all of his dreams too.

I have to say that I was somewhat surprised when Mark reveled in the idea that his beautiful wife sucked down another man's cum in the car. So I decided to give him a show.

Holding back from swallowing, I let Travis pump my mouth with hot seed. He was drained from the blowjob in the car, so I had to be careful to wisely use what wad he gave me now.

I let some of the seed leak out of my locked lips and down my chin. All men loved this, I thought.

As soon as Travis was finished using my mouth to service his cock, I turned and crawled back to Mark on my knees with my mouth open. I pulled myself back onto his lap and let him see all the cum Travis just unloaded. I was just a few inches from his face so he could enjoy the spectacle.

Mark moaned as I swirled my tongue in the cum, looking straight into my eyes as it started to dribble out of my mouth. I swallowed the load and licked my lips as Mark rubbed what was on my face into my skin.

I then wrapped my arms around Mark's head and whispered in his ear.

"Oh God, Mark," I said, "another man just came in my mouth." I licked his ear, adding to the excitement.

"Now he wants to take my cunt to stroke off that big dick of his," I whispered quietly.

"Are you sure you want this man to fuck your wife and make her cum?"

"Not before I do," Mark shot back.

That made sense to me, too. Travis just shot his second wad within a half an hour. I was concerned that the young stud wouldn't be able to get hard again.

Mark got up, forcing me to my feet. In a instant my husband was out of his pants, taking me over to Travis. He pushed my head forward into Travis's lap, hiking my dress so he could fuck me.

I took Travis's limp cock and stuffed it in my mouth as Mark worked his hard cock into my cunt. I immediately started begging Mark for a good hard fuck. The guys didn't even bother to undress me!

"Oh God, I need to feel a hot prick between my legs!" I moaned.

Mark started to stroke me with short strokes, boldly asking Travis questions as he did so.

"My wife gives a good blowjob, doesn't she Travis?"

“Oh man,” Travis said, “you’re so lucky to have such a hot wife!”

I turned around to smile at Mark, but Travis reached around my head and pushed it on his now stiffening cock.

“Yep, this wife of yours sure loves cock, and I bet her tight pussy feels just as good,” Travis replied.

Mark was a sharing man that night.

“You just wait, my friend, my sexy wife is truly one hot, tight fuck.”

He then started humping me faster. And Travis. He wasn’t done telling me what he wanted to do to me.

“You ready for another hard cock when Mark’s done riding you?”

I moaned my acceptance of his offer, my first orgasm hitting me hard. I was more than ready to get fucked by this young stud!

Mark added to the comment.

“He has a pretty big cock, Andrea, can you handle such a big cock?”

I pulled my mouth off from Travis’s cock long enough to turn and answer Mark.

"Fuck me, Oh God, give it to me hard before Travis opens me up with his big cock!"

Mark pumped harder with the statement, grabbing my waist so he could slam his prick into me over and over.

Mark was not an experienced fuck master like Bill or Al. I knew that he couldn't handle the decadent show much longer.

A few short minutes later, I could feel Mark's hot seed spunking up my gash and dripping down my cunt lips. It was the greatest feeling in the world to be used by my husband as another man used my mouth.

By now Travis was a stiff as a board again, ready to experience my cunt. Thank God, I thought!

Travis stood up and striped off his clothes, his big cock sticking out and curving upwards. It was an absolutely beautiful cock, I thought.

I crawled up to him and got up on my knees, taking his cock into my throat one more time. He held the back of my head as he started to force fuck my mouth like a cunt.

Travis fucked my mouth for about five minutes, enjoying the fact that I was easily letting him work his prick in and out of my throat. He then stopped, wrenching his cock out of my throat.

"Now I wanna fuck that nice tight pussy of yours," he said as he pulled me onto the floor with him.

As soon as Travis and I were on the floor, he pushed me on my back. He leaned his body against mine and started to kiss me, running his hand down to my crotch.

I spread my legs for the young stud as his hand went further down. I reveled in the feeling of having my dress hiked up as this strange man tightly gripping my cunt with my husband watching.

Travis continued to kiss me as he withdrew his hand, bringing his body on top of mine. I could notice Mark from the corner of my eye as he intently watched Travis get between my legs to mount me.

I spread my legs wider to take the fresh new cock. Travis slowly entered me. I went crazy feeling the big cock head as it sliced into my horny cunt. God, how I wanted to get fucked again hard!

As Travis pushed the head in, I let out a moan and stopped kissing him to whisper in his ear.

"Ohhhh . . . fuck, Travis," I said.

I looked over towards Mark as I continued talking to Travis, "give me that big hard cock you horny stud."

By now Mark was stroking his cock to another erection, excited by watching his wife begging another man to screw her.

With his head raised so he could look down at me, Travis pushed the long stick further between my legs so everyone could see it going into me. It added immensely to Mark's excitement.

"Oh, Goddamn Mark, your wife's got one helluva tight cunt!" Travis moaned as he mounted me.

Travis pushed the stiff prick into my quivering pussy deeper and deeper, until his cock head was ledged deep inside me.

"Oh, . . . Oh . . . Mark . . . I'm getting laid by this stud's big cock," I moaned to my husband.

Travis and I started kissing again as he began to pump my slick cunt. He took slow short strokes, savoring the feeling of my cunt snapped around his stiff prick.

As Mark's cum started to lubricate his cock more, Travis stopped kissing me to concentrate on the long dicking he was beginning to give me.

Travis pumped furiously between my legs, every now and then expressing his sheer delight as he looked down to see his thick cock stroking between my legs.

"Oh, God, I love your sweet tight cunt," he said over and over.

He went on and on, getting more excited with each stroke of his hard shaft through my pussy.

"You're . . . so . . . fucking hot . . . Andrea," he moaned.

As he talked to me more, the excitement of getting thoroughly laid by this young stud grew within me, too. It was more than I could take.

"Oh fuck, long dick my cunt with that big cock, you stud," I cried.

Looking in Mark's eyes, I said more to assure him that this was all a good thing.

"Fuck, damn, . . . you were right Mark," I said, "I really needed to get laid so bad!!!"

I then drove my heels into the floor so I could use my hips to meet Travis' deep strokes.

"Use my tight cunt to jerk off that thick prick of yours," I moaned as my second orgasm spasmed through me.

Enjoying the word game that was brewing, Travis came back with a perfect reply. Looking at Mark, he told him how it was.

"Ahhhh . . . I'm gonna jerk off a nice load of cum up your wife's sweet, tight cunt Mark!"

Having stroked me for about twenty minutes in this manner, Travis dismounted me and moved behind me. He rolled me over and pushed me onto my side facing Mark.

Travis got behind me and raised me leg. He then took his long cock and began snaking it over my cunt.

"Mmmm . . ." he moaned as he worked the pole back in.

"Suck your husband while I stroke your cunt," he commanded.

By now Mark was hard again, and he came over and laid on the floor in front of me. In a flash I had his cock in my hand,

and I was sucking away like a horny bitch in heat.

As Mark enjoyed his blowjob, Travis started working his cock in and out of me from behind. My dress was hiked enough so Mark could see him taking me, causing him to grow rock hard.

I could feel my mouth open from the joyous feeling between my legs, thoroughly enjoying the long cock as it stroked me cunt in front of my husband. I looked back at Travis and moaned.

"God, Travis, your cock feels so good!" I cooed.

Mark took advantage of my open mouth. He put his hand on the back of my head and pulled it onto his waiting cock. My third orgasm was not far behind.

I could tell that the sight was overwhelming for Mark. He reached down and started tweaking my nipples. Mark then looked at Travis.

"How's my wife's cunt, Travis, what you expected?" Mark asked our guest.

Travis was very intent on humping my cunt, but he did manage to voice his response as he grunted and sweated over my body.

"Oh, damn, she's got one nice cunt," he said, "man you really are one lucky fucker to have a wife like this!"

Damn right, I thought, just as I was lucky to have a husband like Mark. At that point I realized that we really were truly a team.

Travis continued to ride me, and I continued to suck off Mark. I stopped for a minute to look up at Mark and to tell him something he already knew.

"God, Mark, I'm so full of hard cock," I said, immediately slipping his cock back into my throat.

I found that men who already came were able to sport a hard-on for longer periods in subsequent rounds. Travis was no exception. He pumped my cunt for at least 10 minutes.

Travis was eventually getting ready to blow, which caused him to reply to my comment.

". . . and you're gonna get my sticky cum up you're cunt too, baby."

"Give it me," I moaned.

Travis started to grunt and moan, and I could feel his throbbing prick begin to tremble deep in my cunt.

"Oh Fuck, I'm . . . gonna . . . cum . . . deep . . . in your wife's tight . . . cunt! . . . Uggghhh . . ."

I was quick to add to the exciting moment.

"Oh, Mark, I can feel him creaming between my legs."

Mark, too, was caught up in the moment. He surprised me with the newest level of his imagination.

"Ahhh . . . empty our balls you damned slut!"

It was all so exciting, bringing all three of us to as climax at once.

As Travis creamed deep between my legs, Mark blew in my mouth. It was great feeling his cock as it throbbed off in my mouth. An intense orgasm got me too. It ripped through my body, causing me to collapse between Mark's legs.

We all stayed there for a few minutes, Travis twitching against my back from the intensity of his powerful orgasm. I could literally feel the cum dripping out of my cunt and my mouth. We were in heaven.

After a few minutes, Travis' cock finally softened and fell from my cunt. So I got up and fixed my dress as the men looked up and watched me. I went over to the table to grab a quick drink, and then went for my purse.

Pulling out my lipstick and perfume, I seductively put on more in front of my studs. As I pressed my lips together and ran my tongue over them, I looked down and asked if anyone cared for some more.

The men jumped up, both of them taking me into their arms, allowing cum drippings to run down my legs. I kissed each man, back and forth.

I then took the studs by the hands and led them to the bed. I started to slip off my dress as they started to climb on the bed. They were playing with their well-used limp cocks, intently watching my every move.

I stood before them feeling like a decadent whore, reaching behind to unzip my dress. As it feel to the floor, I could see Travis take a deep breath as he saw my big tits pop out before him.

The dress and my shoes were all I had on, so I decided to just leave the heels on. Once the dress was off, I crawled on the bed between the two men. I knew I was in for a ride!

Almost immediately, each went for the tit that was closest. Travis also ran his other hand down to my open, dripping cunt. It was so incredibly erotic to be laying in bed with two men, being felt up by both my husband and a total stranger.

I alternated between the two men, giving them hot wet kisses. My instincts were going wild, and my hands were soon seeking out hot cock to stroke and rub.

We were all having a great time, and it wasn't too long before I had two hard cocks in my hands. I wanted them, now.

"Which of you horny bastards want to slip their cock into me?"

It was an invitation for either man to hump my asshole. I was saddened when there were no takers.

I was somewhat surprised when Travis acted so rude, pushing me around so my ass was in the air. In a flash he was kneeling behind me, pushing his cock up my cunt for the second time that hour. Yes, while Travis was young and clearly inexperienced in ass fucking, he was nevertheless a true stud.

"I'd love to split this tight cunt open again," he said coolly.

I took Mark in my mouth again as Travis began to hump me. Mark reached down and started to feel up my tits while he enjoyed the show.

Travis was a little more lose now that he heard Mark talk to me as he did.

"Fucking slut, Andrea, how does my hard cock feel up your slick tight cunt now?"

I moaned in response, noticing how Mark reveled in the way I was being treated.

"Uggggh, Uggggh, Uggggh . . .," Travis went on as he pumped me.

"Take my hard cock, you beautiful, horny bitch!" he said rudely.

I stopped sucking only to respond. I turned to look at him.

"Slam my cunt, you fucker, give me that big hard cock until I scream!"

Travis obliged, pounding my cunt with such extreme force that I was constantly slammed onto Mark's waiting prick.

Mark pitched in, reaching behind my head to keep the fucking from moving my head away from his cock.

"Suck my cock harder, bitch," he said, "take my cock down your horny throat!"

I did so, deep throating him to the rhythm of the brutal fuck I was getting from Travis.

Both men started to moan.

The spectacle went on for quite a while. The cocks were desensitized from the non-stop fucking, so both were happy to enjoy me.

It took a solid 15 minutes, but I could tell when Travis was ready to blow again. His slams slowed down, but the intensity of the each thrust increased. Travis soon shared his intentions with us.

"Ahhhh fuck, I'm pumping another load up your foxy wife's tight cunt!"

With a grunt and a moan I could feel his cock twitch. There wasn't much of a load to splash my insides, but I didn't care. I loved feeling his hairy ball sack twitch against my asshole.

As soon as Travis got off, Mark was right there to replace him. He quickly jabbed his cock up my cunt with a vengeance.

"You want hot cock, Andrea, here's more hot cock," he said.

Mark then started stroking away as Travis just laid beside us to watch.

Mark banged me for another 10 minutes or so, but it was only a matter of time before he added more seed to mix with the load Travis just injected.

When the fucking was over, the three of us laid there in a heap. We were all pretty drunk and tired by the time we got to that point.

Travis leaned over and kissed me, thanking me for a wonderful time. He then looked at Mark and asked him point blank.

"Man, how did you get such a foxy wife who puts out like this?"

Mark looked a me and smiled.

"I'm just a lucky man," he said, "I married the most incredible woman in the world!"

I was quick to interject.

"Actually, I love Mark more than anything in the world, and I would do anything to satisfy any need he has."

It was a deal for any man, and I wanted Mark to know that.

Travis agreed.

“Oh fuck, you lucky bastard,” he said, “I hope I find a beautiful wife like yours!”

“You will,” I whispered back, “just give it time.”

I was ready to talk to Mark about our little experience, to see if it was a success that we would be repeating many times in the future. But I had to get rid of Travis.

I got up and slipped on my dress. I thanked Travis for a wonderful time and asked him for his phone number. I think he got the message, as he dressed and gave me a big kiss goodbye. I walked him to the door and off he went, no doubt a very happy young man.

I locked the door and went back to the bed. I got under the covers and held Mark by the chest. There was silence for the longest time as Mark caressed my body with his warm hands.

I had to know what he was thinking.

My voice rang out.

“So, what did you think?” I asked my husband.

Mark said it was exciting, but he admitted that it took him a while to get used to seeing another man have me.

Mark said he didn't know how he felt when he saw me sucking and then fucking a stranger. He had to fight the jealousy, he said, but it excited him a great deal. He then admitted that he was afraid he might lose me if I liked it too much or found someone better.

I understood completely. I knew it would only be a matter of time before he would want another woman to join us. How would I handle it? That was a problem for another day, I thought.

I reassured Mark that he was the only man for me, and that I was deeply in love with him – more so, in fact, now that we were beginning to share each other sexually. We affirmed that we would never be with another person unless the other agreed and was there. It was a promise I resolved to myself that I would keep. My marriage and family were just too important to jeopardize.

Mark and I decided to stay in the motel room that night since our daughters were with their grandparents. All night I dreamed of hard cock, always picturing Mark beside me as I took a new beast between my legs. My mind was subconsciously crying out for more cock!

The next morning I awoke to find Mark caressing my back. He asked how I felt, and I told him I felt wonderful.

I was like a new woman, I said. I was so happy that I fulfilled his desires, and at the same time found that I, too, truly loved the feel of open sex.

We then talked some more.

I got Mark to discuss the dirty talk that went on. He said he loved the way I talked, which was a relief.

Mark then apologized for calling me dirty names and for letting Travis make vile remarks to me. I reminded him of the ground rules, that the guest could do or so anything that was not truly bizarre. I paused for a moment. Besides, I added, it was all just a part of the act to really arose everyone.

Mark smiled and kissed me, clearly appreciating my response.

I was surprised when Mark eventually confessed that he actually thought the whole thing wasn't nasty enough!

I asked him if he wanted to try this again. He said he did. Next time, I vowed, I would act worse.

Mark smiled and kissed me.

"You are so wonderful," he said.

"And you are too, my husband," I responded.

As soon as Mark said that he wanted it even worse, my mind immediately thought of Al.

My big Mandingo stud.

That black bastard was a cocksman and a half, and he was the most vile sexual partner I had experienced in my brief but intense travels. Damn I missed Al!

I thought about setting something up with Al, but I was so afraid that he was too arrogant to keep my dangerous secret of the black gang bang. It could ruin my marriage if Mark found out.

Yes, it was certainly a risk, but I knew Al was the one we needed to truly open Mark's sexual awareness. Even though I never did test out his honesty, he had agreed to end the gang bang if I told him to and he did protect me.

I knew Al would be genuinely interested in seeing me again. But could he live with some grounds rules, I wondered. I resolved to find out.

Looking back at Mark, I answered his one comment of disappointment.

"I think so, sweetheart," I said, "the next one will be more nasty!"

He smiled.

Chapter 33

Mark and I had great fun together. We fucked the rest of the week and into the weekend, discussing our experience with Travis and what our next time would be like.

There was no doubt that this was a new "family activity" for us, and I must admit that I was thrilled that it truly was a family activity. I had no desire to cheat on the man I loved so much.

It was as though I was redeemed by a higher power, and I vowed that no matter what I would never break our rule about being with other people without the knowledge and participation of the other.

The more I thought about my incredible luck, the more delirious I got. We both had similar desires. What were the odds of that happening in a marriage, especially in the hypocritical society in which we live?

And Mark. He apparently has had these thoughts the whole time. More than once I wondered how our marriage would have gone if Bill hadn't ruined me.

It was time for the next step.

The more I thought about it, the more I came to the conclusion that there was one man who really moved me. Al. I had been with many men up to this point, and he was by far the best lover I've ever had.

And that magnificent cock!

I loved that black cock more than any other tool I've had the pleasure of meeting except – maybe – Jamar's great brown cock. Yes, it was a close tie, but Jamar was clearly a sexist rich man who would be absolutely uncontrollable.

I found myself thinking thought about Al more and more. Everything about him was sexually compatible with me, from his body to his attitude. And I will never forget how he defended me against Eddie, and how he treated me with kindness as he orchestrated the use my body by his friends. I will also never forget his son, Nickie. What a perfect young gentleman he was.

In retrospect, Al was like an ebony God to my body, and I knew his son was not far behind! Yes, I thought, I wanted it to be Al. But there were so many questions that flooded my mind.

How could I find him?

Did I keep that number he gave to me?

Would he keep my secret of how I became an unbridled slut?

And what about Mark? How would he feel about a black man scoring with me?

By this time, Mark had started to bring home some porn movies. We watched them intently, Mark often commenting how I was better looking and more skilled than the porn queens we saw.

The porn was a new experience for me. Here I was, a church-going married woman with two small daughters. But damn! They made me so wet! They even taught me new tricks.

I saw the porn as an opportunity. I got on the Internet and found a porn web site. It didn't take much effort to find movies of anal sex and black men in a menage a trois. I especially like the *Screw My Wife* videos. Fantastic!

Mark was surprised when I handed him one of the movies. He asked me if I wanted to try anal sex as we watched the movies. I told him Mark that I found the idea intriguing based on how the porn stars clearly enjoyed it so much. So I told him I would think about the idea. I didn't want him to know that I was already an ass slut.

And then there were the movies with black studs. The Lex vs Mandingo series really, really turned me on. You have to admire Ava Scott. She is so beautiful and talented. What an inspiration for me!

As he watched the movies, Mark asked me if I liked black men. I hated to lie, but I told him I didn't know. I told him that it was such a taboo, that I found the idea kind of exciting.

I watched to see his reaction. To my great surprise, he seemed fine with it.

So we watched the movies. Mark was amazed.

"Damn!" he said, "I wonder if that Lex Steele's cock is considered normal?!?!?"

Lex Steele looked a lot like Al, I thought. No hair, very muscular, dark skinned, and a massive log between his legs. I couldn't help but respond enticingly to Mark.

"I don't know," I said, "but do you remember when you said I could handle ANY cock?"

I continued as he smiled.

"Do you think you could handle seeing that cock stroking off in me?"

Mark smiled again and leaned over to kiss me. He gently ran his hand up my thigh.

"I'd love to see that sweetheart," he said, "but only if you want to."

Boy, did I!

"You know," I said, "I really would kinda like to see what's it's like to get laid by a black man."

Mark nodded, as though he was open to the whole idea.

I thought about it some more, and I was ready to make a proposition to him. I had practiced it over and over in my mind. How to introduce Al to our relationship.

"Hey," I said, "there's a black man who comes to the bank every week. He's a good customer, and I see him looking me up and down every time he comes in."

Mark looked at me with a puzzled look, as if he was wondering if I was having an affair with the black man.

"I don't really know him," I quickly added, "but he seems to be very nice and upstanding whenever he talks to me."

"Well," Mark said, "do you think it would hurt your job?"

I thought for a moment.

"No," I said, "perhaps just find a way to invite the man to lunch with you and me. I'm sure I can find something common between us with some casual conversation."

"Well, ok Andrea," Mark responded, "if you can do it without causing yourself trouble."

The following Monday I went to work with a new enthusiasm. I was on top of the world, a woman set free to enjoy her sexuality under the watchful gaze of her husband.

I set my mind to the next "guest," Al, and whether he would be willing to cooperate. It had been so long.

I searched everywhere for his phone number for over a week. I was going nuts! But I finally found the number buried in a coat in my closet.

I picked up the phone at work the following Monday. I nervously dialed his number. he black stud was obviously a little startled to hear my voice after more than a year since our one-night encounter.

I told Al that I wanted to meet and talk. I asked if he would be interested in seeing me again. I knew the horny bastard would, so I wasn't surprised when he agreed to meet me for lunch that day. But I had business meetings the next few days, so it had to wait until Friday.

All that week I quivered with anticipation! How would it go? What would Al say?

Al and I met at a small diner close to the bank. I found him waiting there in a booth promptly at noon. This was a good sign, I thought. He was very interested.

I walked over to Al and sat down across from him. He leaned over the booth, clearly wanting to give me a kiss. I hesitated for a moment, in case once of my hypocritical co-workers was in the diner. I backed off from him.

Al didn't like it.

"So, what's up? You call me hear and won't even give me a kiss?"

I immediately set the stage.

"Look Al, I'm married, and I love my husband," I told him.

"What I do to take care of my needs and those of my friends is nobody's business, and I don't care to share it with the world."

Al apologized, apparently understanding what I was saying. He went on with another remark.

"So, can't get enough of Al's black cock, huh?"

I told him that such an attitude was fine when sex was involved, but he needed to treat me with a little respect if he ever wanted to see me again.

I paused for a moment and then made it clear that there were plenty of men who would love to be with me. I didn't need to be with an arrogant bastard.

Al hung his head sheepishly, as if he was kind of embarrassed. I decided to let up a bit. I didn't want to drive the man away.

I explained to Al about that day when he laid me, and what happened. I told him all about how I was opened up sexually, and that I just couldn't control my urges. I added that I loved it, but that I had to keep my marriage together.

"So then what happened," he asked.

I explained about Mark's fantasy, and how we tried it out. I made it quite clear that I was Mark's slut, but that I could get him to share me with whomever I wanted.

Al was all ears.

"So, how can I help?" he asked.

I explained to him that we needed to find a third partner, someone we could trust and rely on. A person who would really enjoy what he was getting, and someone who wasn't afraid to talk as filthy as his mind could conceive.

Al listened intently, obviously wanting to be that man.

I told Al if he kept my secret and respected my husband, I might be willing to be his regular fuck as long as Mark was with us.

It obviously made Al very happy to hear all of this, as he gave me a devilish grin. My God, how often would he get the chance to fuck a gorgeous married white woman with her husband? And maybe – just maybe – regularly?!?

When I was finished, Al said he understood and that he would love to help us. With that I set out the one ground rule, that he would do everything in his power to keep secret that night I had met him and his buddies. Al readily agreed.

I also made sure that I explained how important it was that Mark like him. Al certainly could not be the regular third person if Mark did not like him. He understood.

When we finished, we agreed that we would "bump into" each other this a week from Saturday at the same night club Mark and I had gone to the previous Saturday. That would give me time to work on Mark.

I didn't know whether I could really trust Al or not, but I wanted to give it a try. I felt it was worth the risk.

Al made me feel more comfortable as we walked out of the diner.

"So, I can talk any way I want to?" he asked.

My reply was brief and to the point.

"Yes, as long as you keep the secret," I warned him.

"If you don't," I added, "you'll never fuck me again!"

I knew my young, white married ass I was the best fuck Al ever had in his life. I had no doubt about that fact. And I knew Al missed the best fuck of his life since last year.

Al understood that his long-lost white prize was now going to be back in his bed – whenever he wanted if he played his cards right. I knew in my heart Al would not jeopardize losing his lusty whore.

My belief was soon affirmed.

"Don't worry, Andrea," he said.

"I told you last year I'd take care of you, and I still mean it."

Al smiled as he told me not to worry, clearly wanting to kiss me. I smiled back, saying that I would see him on Saturday. I blew him a kiss, turned and walked away.

I was anxious all that week. I wanted so much to be filled with Al's big black cock and to taste his cum, but at the same time I was scared that he would screw me by telling Mark.

My mind raced.

Would he do that? He must know I would never see him again if he did.

Time ended the worry. A week from Saturday night arrived before I knew it.

Chapter 34

Mark and I talked a lot about our next sexual adventure throughout the week. I told him I really wanted to go to a night club again just to feel like a beautiful, desirable woman.

The kids were going to be at their grandparents again on the upcoming weekend, so Mark said he didn't mind. I suggested the same club as last time, and he agreed.

Mark remembered our last arrangement. He got to pick the last man I fucked, and I got to pick this one.

"What if I pick a black man?" I grinned.

"If you want to try it, sweetheart," he said, "it's ok with me."

"Are you sure?" I asked, "they have pretty big cocks."

"If you want to handle a big cock, Andrea, then I wanna see it," he responded.

Great! It was all set. Working Al into the arrangement shouldn't be a problem.

I put a great deal of thought as to how I would look. I wanted to look absolutely perfect!

Mark and I agreed that I shouldn't use my red "fuck" outfit this time. It was just too revealing and created problems last time. It drew every horny asshole to me like a magnet, which ruined a lot more of the evening that we cared for.

We decided I would wear a short, sexy skirt with a low-cut blouse. Mark was hoping that a gentleman would see me and appreciate what opportunity was before him. I thought about it and came to one conclusion. I wore the same outfit Bill took me in.

Next question. Bare leg or hose? That was a tough one. I liked to get fucked wearing hose, but bare leg was also extremely sexy. What the hell, I thought. Men go crazy with hose, so hose it was. Now, what kind?

I always remembered my lesson with the stockings Bill gave me. They were clearly visible when I sat at the bar stool in a short skirt. So I decided on white pantyhose. Crotchless, of course!

Should I wear a bra? No, I decided. While I knew I had big tits and large nipples that would definitely stick out, it was a trade off. I didn't want to be hampered when the action started.

I dressed up in my outfit, making sure to wear heels with a strap. Al was a ruthless fuck monster, and I didn't want them to go flying off hitting someone! Besides, I absolutely loved getting fucked in heels. In fact, it seems that I always had heels on when men took me.

I also had my hair and nails done professionally that morning. I added to it with a perfect make-up job that evening, dark eye shadow and my red lip stick.

I slipped on the string of pearls Bill spunked up and my wedding rings, a quick splash of sexy perfume, and we were ready to go!

When we walked into the night club it was obvious that the horny reaction was not the same. Sure, men looked at me and wondered how I'd be in the sack, but it wasn't the same.

I think Mark was right. I hadn't gone in an outfit that advertised that I was there to get fucked. I could have been any professional woman going in with her husband for a few drinks and some dancing.

Mark and I went a little earlier to make sure we could get a good seat. It was very packed last time and we only lucked out.

Well, we lucked out again. The people sitting at the table we had last time got up and left as we walked around the room checking out the men.

As he did last time, Mark left me at the table while he went to get drinks. Things were a little different this time, though. I knew who I was going home with. I just needed to get Mark to by into the "random" selection of Al. At least this night it was my turn to chose!

We had gotten there a little earlier than I told Al, so I had to do my best to act interested in my suitors until he arrived and I could find a way to meet him. I danced with three men as I kept up the charade, one of them being so bold as to feel up my ass.

Even Travis appeared, no doubt looking for a repeat with me. I made it clear to Mark that I wanted to try someone new, so he did not try to get me to sleep with Travis again. I hope I didn't hurt Travis' feelings, but I promised we would meet him again some other time.

Like clockwork, Al was on time.

I saw my black stud walk by, catching the glance he gave to me. He was certainly dressed to kill, and I lusted for him the instant I saw him.

I immediately got up, telling Mark that I had to go to the women's room. I followed Al as he went to the bar, a crowd of people blocking Mark's view of us.

I walked up to Al and quickly told him how we would do it. I then went back to the table and sat with Mark.

About ten minutes later as a slow song commenced, Al strolled up to our table as planned and said hello. The plan was to indicate to Mark that I already knew him from the bank.

"Hi Al," I said, "how are you?"

I then looked at Mark and told him who this strange black man was.

"Honey, you remember Al," I said.

"He's the customer from the bank that I told you about a few weeks ago."

Mark was quick to catch on. Not knowing that Al was my pre-ordained fuckmate for the night, he was casual about it.

"Hi Al," he said, "it's nice to meet you."

Al didn't waste any time. He only talked for a few minutes and then made his move.

"Mark, my man," he said, "you have a beautiful wife and a talented banker there!"

I smiled sheepishly as Mark looked at Al and accepted the compliment for me.

"Yes," Mark responded, "she's the best wife a man could ask for."

Al continued his move, not about to be deprived of his score for the night due to any misunderstandings.

Would you mind if I asked Andrea to dance?" he asked Mark.

I could see that Mark was pleased that this new man was so polite to ask his permission.

"Be my guest," he said, "Andrea loves to dance."

Mark then looked at me, giving me permission to do the same.

"Go ahead Andrea," he said, "feel free to dance with Al if you'd like."

Al took my hand and helped me from the bar stool. He put his arm around my waist, and we walked off to the dance floor.

Al and I danced to two songs. It was incredible that he remained a perfect gentlemen as planned. He held my hands like a gentleman while we danced, and we only talked.

I must say that it felt wonderful being next to this black stud again. And I was very impressed with the way he was behaving.

When the songs were done, Al walked me back to the table and thanked Mark. He then left as planned so Mark and I could talk.

Mark didn't say anything, but was clearly a little distraught. I leaned over to him and whispered in his ear as I grabbed his crotch.

"Are you sick from the thought of a big buck nigger taking me?" I whispered.

Mark said that he didn't know. He asked me if I liked this man. I said he was always very nice at the bank, and that he was a perfect gentleman when he danced with me. I thought it was refreshing, I explained. I quickly added that I hadn't made any decisions on who I was going to sleep with that night.

Mark was obviously relieved, and it underscored that I was right in handling him as gently as I was.

About twenty minutes later, Al came back as planned. He immediately started to strike up a conversation.

Al stood the whole time as we talked for about fifteen minutes. Al turned out to be quite a conversationalist. What a relief is was to me that him and Mark had interests in common.

When another slow number came up, Al politely asked Mark if he could dance with me again. Mark said that would be fine.

I whispered in Mark's ear.

"Do I take this to the next step love?" I asked.

Mark gave me a little smile and reluctantly nodded his head with approval.

Al and I danced again. This time I invited him to take me into his strong arms. I felt so comfortable being next to my black stud. I had to resist kissing him until his position in our bed was solidified.

Al was also having a tough time, obviously fighting to keep his hands off my ass. He casually rubbed my back instead. But we did dance very close the entire time.

When the set of songs were over, we went back to the table. I asked Al if he would like to join us, which he readily accepted. He came around and sat in the seat next to me.

Mark seemed a little uncomfortable again, but I think he relaxed as we all talked and drank some more. I hoped he would agree that Al could come home with us.

About twenty minutes later, Al excused himself to go to the men's room. As soon as he left, Mark quickly told me his impression.

"That black man really wants to fuck you," he said.

I moved closer to him and smiled.

"I always wondered about blacks, haven't you?, I said, "Don't you want to know if those movies are real?"

Mark looked at me and spoke with an urgency.

"Yeah, but why such an old one?"

My answer was concise.

"Why not try an older one? Black and old are both so taboo. It's kind of exciting. Besides, an older man may have some real experience -- this might be the nastier experience you are looking for!"

Mark knew that my sights were set on Al, but he continued to try to talk me out of it.

"You know, that black guy in the movie had a really big cock," he said. "What if this guy has one too? Can you really handle it?"

I leaned over and kissed him and then whispered in his ear.

"Can you handle it?" I asked him rhetorically.

Mark looked at me and told me that he wanted me to be happy, and that he would try to get used to what I wanted to do. Besides, he said, it might be fun seeing me opened by a big black dick.

I thanked him with a kiss and made the announcement.

"Ok, then," I said, "I choose Al."

"If that's your choice love," Mark responded, "ok."

When Al came back, he sat down a little closer to me. I needed to find a way to show him that the decision was made.

As we talked and drank, I moved closer and closer to Al. We joked, and I would rub his arm with my hand. Mark didn't say a word, a clear signal to Al that my advances were welcome by my husband.

Al responded in due course. He started putting his arm around me when he would tell a joke. Eventually, his hand moved under the table. Mark could tell what he was doing, I was sure.

The black stud ran his hand up my skirt and rubbed my legs, feeling my pantyhose. Mark didn't say a word.

As we talked some more, Al got more daring in his bid to feel me up. He soon had his hand moving between my legs, which I parted to allow him access to my cunt. I could tell from his gaze that Mark could see Al's arm moving under the table.

I pulled out my lipstick and slowly started to put it on. Mark knew that I was signaling that I was almost ready to leave, intent on taking this black man into my bed to stud me.

We continued to talk and drink a bit more as Al felt me up. He was clearly enjoying what he was doing to me in front of my husband. I couldn't really tell how Mark was feeling about it. The tension was broken when Al asked me to dance again.

When we got out to the dance floor, Al was more forceful. This time he openly went for my ass. hiking my skirt until the whole dance floor could see that I had on crotchless pantyhose and no panties. Al was really getting into it, stroking my ass with his large black hands for the public to see.

Al and I then started to kiss, his tongue probing mine. I was lost is heaven, wishing this big black stud could take me right there on the dance floor. I felt so lose and like such a slut, letting this beast so blatantly feel me up and kiss me in public.

My mind then turned to Mark, who was surely watching me. When the slow number finished, Al walked me back to the table and immediately headed for the men's room. When he was gone, Mark made a few comments to me.

"Did you like being felt up on the dance floor by him?"

I smiled and looked down innocently, and then I looked up at him. I took a guess and asked him a question.

“Did you like watching that black stud man-handling your wife?”

“It was kind of exciting,” he admitted.

I pushed it a step further.

“You’ve always wanted to see a big black man take me, haven’t you Mark?”

The beer was definitely making its presence known as his inhibitions had fallen.

“Well, sure, who wouldn’t want to see his wife get laid by a big black stud?”

I moved close to whisper in his ear.

“Mark, love, would you be OK if your wife got laid by a big black stud?” I asked.

Our heads turned and we kissed. I grabbed his hand and brought it up my skirt to my wet cunt. I spread my legs wide for him as he started to feel me up. I wanted him to see how excited this all made me.

As Mark and I kissed, Al came back and sat down. He watched us kiss for a few minutes and then pipped in his thoughts.

"Andrea sure is a beautiful woman Mark, but you'll get to do that when you go home."

Mark stopped and looked at Al.

It was time for the invitation.

"Is that what you were thinking out on the dance floor Al?"

I've found that Al always had a witty response ready.

"I'm really sorry, Mark, but she is such a captivating woman," he said kindly, " I just couldn't resist when she was in my arms."

Mark smiled, obviously pleased that the man appreciated me.

Everyone knew at that point that the deal was just about sealed. Giving up his last reservations, Mark looked at Al and asked him the fatal question.

"So, Al, do you want to sleep with my wife?"

Al came close to me and wrapped his arm around me. He reached in front of me and ran his hand under my skirt so he could feel Mark's hand. He cupped Mark's hand and push it with his against my cunt. What a feeling!

"As a matter of fact," he said, "I would be grateful to share such a beautiful lady with you."

With that I turned and kissed Al, reaching over to rub Mark's crotch.

I told the men what I wanted.

"Fuck, I've always wanted to get laid by a big black stud!"

Al has a quick reply.

"Well here's your chance baby!"

I turned and whispered in Mark's ear.

"He's an upstanding bank customer," I said, "I think it's ok if we bring him to the house."

Mark agreed, accepting my view of the situation.

We went out to the parking lot. Al followed us to our house.

Chapter 35

When we got to the house, Mark held my hand as we walked to the door.

"Are you sure you want to do this?" he asked.

"Are you sure you want me to do it?" I responded.

We both smiled and walked to the door. We knew the answers.

Al was parking on the street and was coming up behind us as we opened the door. As soon as we got to in, Mark took me by the hand into the kitchen. He asked Al to pick out some music from our CDs. I guess jazz is the music of sex, as Al also picked out some light jazz.

As soon as we were in the kitchen, Mark again asked me if I really wanted to go through with this. I guess he was really hesitant about breaking the taboo of interracial sex.

I paused for a moment and then told him that I did – for both of us. He nodded. I reassured him that it would be ok. That it was time to make his dream come true, and for me to grow sexually.

As we started to walk back to the living room, Mark stopped behind me and put his arms around me. He started to ask what we would do if . . . I didn't let him finish the statement.

"Remember the rule we set up when I decided to put out to other men for you," I said, "the guest gets to do or say anything he wants as long as its not bizarre or weird."

Mark knew that I was doing this for him, and he nodded his reaffirmation of our basic agreement.

"I'm scared," he said quietly, "I don't want to lose you."

I suppose he was worried about those stories of white women who become enthralled with a black man. I felt for the man who I loved so much, and I knew the sights he was about to see could hurt him. He had no idea what Al was about to do to me right in front of him.

I turned to look into his eyes, holding his face with my hands.

"Mark, this is for you," I told him.

"I want to be what you want me to be, and I'm being submissive to your needs."

Mark looked down.

I reassured him again.

"It's just sex, Mark," I said, "and that's all it will ever be."

He was still sullen.

"I'll always love you, I'll never leave you, and I'll never let anyone hurt you if I can help it. So be submissive yourself, and just enjoy the show. It'll be alright."

I then took him by the hand and walked back into the living room. It was time to show him.

Once back in the living room, Mark went to his recliner. Al was still putting on the music, so I handed him a beer and went to sit on Mark's lap.

When Al was finished, he sat down on the brick fireplace. The three of us then talked a little about sex to break the ice.

"Andrea, you ever been with a black man?" he asked.

What a question! He must have known that I had to lie, but I was worried that the fucker was breaking our deal.

"No," I said sheepishly, "I haven't."

"Mmmm, I think you're in for a real treat then, wouldn't you say Mark?"

Al quickly added something to reassure Mark.

"You sure you're ok with this man?"

Mark looked down and nodded, not being able to add a line in my defense.

"Actually, Mark, I think you're in for a treat."

Mark smiled at the comment, taking a sip of his beer.

"Andrea, I couldn't help but notice your beauty all night," Al said to me. "How 'bout showing us a little more?"

I put my head on Mark's shoulder, slowly hiking my dress to show Al my legs.

"Mmm, Mmm," he said, "they sure are fine legs!"

Al could obviously see the seams of my white crotchless pantyhose, surely not a surprise given the way he felt me up at the bar. He let us know about his knowledge.

"I sure like those pantyhose you have on," he said.

With that comment I raised my skirt to my waist, exposing the thick black bush of my naked pussy.

I started running my long red fingernails through the hair surrounding my cunt, spreading my cuntal lips as I did so. It was a sight Al clearly loved.

"Mmmm, look at the thick black bush on that pretty young wife of yours," he told my husband. "Mark, you're quite a lucky man," he added.

By now Mark was getting horny, watching this black man eye my wares. He started to reach around in front of me, feeling up my tits through my blouse. Al smiled as Mark cupped and rubbed my tits, suggesting the next course of action.

"Let those poor nipples out," he said, "why don't you make it easy for them?"

I took Al's advice, and slowly unbuttoned my blouse about three quarters of the way. I then pulled my blouse around my large mounds, letting them stick out for Al's viewing pleasure.

Once my tits were out, Mark started rubbing them and then tweaking my nipples, making them rise and stand out more. My fire was beginning to ignite as Al commented again.

"Yes sir, you gotta wife that men would die for!"

Mark then reached down between my legs with one of his hand. I spread my legs so Mark could feel me up – and to let Al see my hairy slit. Mark replied to Al.

"This is what men would die for, isn't it Andrea?"

I turned to smile at him, giving him a kiss as he felt me up. Al replied to Mark.

"Oh, look at this lips!" he said, "Those are a fine set of pussy lips!"

I was getting horny from the attention these men were giving me, my pussy and tits totally exposed. Al watched, taking in the sight of Mark feeling me up.

"I bet it's tight as hell, isn't it?" Al asked.

"You'll find out soon enough," I said to him with a grin.

Al smiled and stood up. He walked over to me and kneeled down. He went down on me.

As Al started licking my clit, I was going nuts. Mark squeezed my tits as a french kissed him. I reached down and started rubbing Al's bald head.

"Ohhhh . . . ," I moaned.

Al continued working on my cunt for a good five more minutes. He worked his fingers into my cunt and rubbed my clit. I moaned the whole time.

"Yes sir're," Al said, "this pretty wife of yours has a VERY tight pussy!"

I rubbed his head harder when I heard his words.

"You think she can take a big black cock up here?" he asked, as if he gave a shit how we answered.

We both remained silent as he continued to eat me out. Mark and I just kept kissing. Suddenly, Al stopped and stood up.

"Well, then, Andrea, you ready to experience some black cock?"

Was I ever!

I got up off from Mark and stood up. I let Al take me in his arms. He wrapped his arms around me, bringing his hand up my skirt to grip my ass cheeks. He then kissed me, which I hungrily returned.

A few seconds later, Al stopped kissing me and put his strong hands on my shoulders. He pushed me down, clearly an instruction for me to get on my knees.

"You like to suck cock, sweetheart?" he asked as he pushed me down on my knees.

I nodded sheepishly that I did.

"Then go ahead, try a black one," he said.

I let my hands slid down his chest to his legs. I reached up and slowly unzipped his pants. Mark was mesmerized the whole time. He never took his eyes off the spectacle of his pretty young wife unzipping a big buck nigger's pants.

I reached in to Al's pants and grabbed a hold of his limp black snake. I yanked it out through the fly, and immediately started jacking it.

"It sure is black," I said innocently.

"It will compliment that fine white mouth," he quickly snapped back as he brought his hand to the back of my head.

I opened my mouth and let Al guide it to the massive cock head that hung before me. I sucked on the big head, feeling the cock stiffen in my hand.

I tried to look up into Al's face as I pulled it out of my mouth to lick up and down the great shaft, each time popping the head into my mouth.

It was an incredible experience feeling the black fuck stick swell to unreal proportions while my husband watched.

As it grew more and more, I took it out of my mouth so Mark could see it. I leaned back and held it out.

"I guess those porn movies were true," I said to my husband.

"Oh fuck, . . ." was all he could say.

Al's hot prick was soon as stiff as a board, sticking out like a club ready to beat a white woman. I reached up and squeezed my tits together, letting Al push the black cock between them.

As soon as Al was truly hard, he backed away from me. I leaned back on my elbows to watch him as he unbuckled his pants and dropped them to the floor. He stripped down to nothing, leaving that huge monster sticking out.

Al's cock was an incredible sight. A tall, older black man with muscular arms and legs, a thick black log sticking straight out.

I looked back at Mark and smiled, but he was too entranced by the size of the cock that was about to take his wife to notice.

Al moved over to sit on the couch, grabbing me by the hand as he walked past me. I followed the black stud and sat next to him, taking his big cock in my hand.

I looked at Mark and asked permission.

"Mark, love, do you mind if I suck Al's cock some more?"

Mark smiled and nodded his approval. Thank God, he was starting to get into it! So I added to the spectacle.

"Quite a cock, isn't it Mark?" I asked.

He nodded again as he started to laugh.

Al joined in the conversation.

"You sure you want me to fuck your sweet wife with my big black cock?, he asked.

Mark was still a little stunned, and he couldn't answer. I think reality was starting to sink in as the alcohol started to wear off. He eventually to mumbled a reply.

"How big is that thing?" Mark asked.

Al was proud to tell him as I started jerking it.

"Fourteen inches of black rock, and so thick your wife can't even get her hand around it!"

Al went on.

"How 'bout more of that blowjob, sweetheart?" he asked.

I leaned over and took the great fuck stick in my mouth, not for an instant stopping the furious jerking off I was giving it.

Mark was still amazed.

"That thing has to be the size of Lex Steele's," he said.

Al felt insulted.

"Lex Steele ain't got nothin' on me, man!" he retorted.

The talk was getting me hotter. I sucked the head in as far as I could, letting it stretch my mouth all out of proportion. I made sure Mark could see it push out against the side of my mouth.

"Maybe not," Mark said in a quiet voice.

I bobbed my head up and down on the massive fuck stick more. Al just rubbed his fingers through my hair, commenting the whole time to Mark.

“Your wife sure is a hot little cocksucker!” Al jeered to Mark.

I moaned in response, stopping my bobbing to vent my approval..

“I love a big cock in my mouth,” I said.

I then lifted the shaft to lick the huge hairy ball sac underneath it. I then brought my head back up to the massive cock head and reinserted it into my mouth as Al capitalized on the crude talk.

“Your wife sure talks like a little tramp,” he said.

“Yeah, she can be a real slut,” Mark responded.

I reached down to rub Al’s balls with my long nails, and I finally heard him moan for the first time. I stopped sucking for a moment to rub my tits up and down his throbbing cock. I loved the feel of a hard, hot prick against my tits.

Al loved it as much as I did.

“That’s it baby, stroke my big prick with those huge titties!” he said.

It was too exciting for him. I knew that he would soon want to feel something tight on his cock. My pussy was ready, but

Al was intent on using my throat first. Oh God, Mark was about to see me deep throat a massive black cock!

Al put his hand on the back of my head as I tried to work more of the shaft into my mouth. He then pushed down, forcing his cock into my throat.

I could hear Mark gasp.

Instantly remembering what Bill had told me, I relaxed as much as I could. The thick black snake then wormed it s way into my throat. Al's cock was truly too large to deep throat. I got most of it in, but I just couldn't take the rest.

As soon as felt the head so deep that it was stretching my throat, I clamped my mouth shut on the shaft with as much energy as I could, forcing my head up.

Al tried to hold me there, but I think he realized that this was not the time to upset the apple cart. He relaxed his grip and let my head come up.

I then pushed my head back down on the shaft, voluntarily letting it embed itself back into my throat. Al looked at Mark and asked him a question.

"You ever see her do that to a cock my size?"

Mark was amazed at what I was doing. His eyes were as big as golf balls! But Mark was proud of me, and he let it show.

"Andrea loves to suck cock, no doubt about it!"

Al added a crude rebuttal.

"Yeap, she sure knows how to give good head to nigger cock!"

I continued deep throating Al for about five minutes, my sore mouth more than ready to stop when Al pulled my head up to his. The black stud put his arm around me and kissed me.

"OK, Mark, your sweet little wife sure can handle a big black cock in that hot mouth of hers," he said. "Now let's see how that hot little pussy you were bragging about feels!"

"Oh God, . . . ," I cried out. "I don't know Al, you're so big."

"I'll lube you up a little more baby," he said, "don't worry."

The Mandingo stud knelt down and push me onto my back. He hiked up my skirt and spread my legs with his strong black hands. In a flash he was between them, licking at my hairy cunt again.

I went wild! The feeling of the nigger's tongue darting over my clit and nibbling on my cunt lips was overwhelming. It caused the first of many orgasms I would have that night.

"Ohhhhhhhh . . . God," I slowly moaned.

"Lick my pussy Al, suck on my hairy pussy!" I cried out.

Al licked my cunt like that for about five minutes. He flicked his tongue over my clit while his big black fingers pulled on my cuntal lips. I kept moaning it felt so good.

I unbuttoned the rest of my blouse as Al spread held my legs open with one of his hands. I wanted Mark to see my big tits bouncing around from the brutal fucking I was about to get.

As Al ate me, Mark came up and got down on the floor next to me. He gave me a deep loving french kiss. While Mark and I kissed, Al's rough hands came up and started kneading my naked big tits.

After Al made me cum again, he stopped and looked up at Mark. Now it was the moment of truth. Al told him my husband what was next.

"That's one tasty pussy, my man, now let's see what it does to a hard black cock."

Finally! Al was ready to lay me.

Al crawled between my legs and positioned himself to mount me. Mark watched intently. Then Al stopped. He must have remembered that Mark never answered his earlier question.

"Well, Mark?" he asked. "Can you handle watching me bang the hell out of your foxy little wife?"

Al didn't wait for Mark to answer. As soon as his question came out of his mouth, he grabbed my waist and literally pulled me into the massive cock head. He quickly had me impaled on the first few inches of his magnificent black cock.

As the cockhead split my cunt lips open to accept the black shaft, my eyes looked at Mark and grew large as my mouth popped open. I immediately let lose with a low, throaty moan.

Al paused for a moment, looked at Mark and grinned.

"Good!" he answered for Mark.

Al then took his great cock in his hand to start his big snake up my cuntal passage.

The master cocksman worked the massive prick into my cunt a few inches, letting it get juiced up with my cum.

"Damn Andrea," he said coldly, "you're cunt sure is tight!"

I was pretty wet by then, so I think his comment was more for show. I played along, let out another slow moan for Mark to enjoy.

As soon as the head and about 3 inches of his prick were thoroughly imbedded between my legs, Al had another remark.

"Dude, I hate to tell you this . . ." he said with a pause. "But your wife has a big black dick stuck in her cunt!"

That really helped to break the ice. Both men laughed as Al started to stroke me with the few inches of his cock to help lube it up.

"Man, you wife's cunt's tight," he said again as he worked in more and more of his cock.

"I know," said Mark, "she's only been with 2 other men."

Oh God! If he only knew!

Al smiled and looked at me.

"Is that right, baby?"

"That's right," I quickly said back with a smile.

Al then pushed the head in even further, until about 6 inches of his coke-can rod was stuffed up my cunt. Here was Al, stretching my cunt wide open with his big black cock in full view of my stunned husband.

When he was about 8 inches in, he stopped again to ask another question.

"You ever had a cock this deep into you baby?"

All I could do was moan and nod my head back and forth.

"Time to make love to your beautiful wife," Al then said as he pushed the giant cock head further into me.

The sensation drew a deep lusty moan from within me.

Al then straightened his body and started to ride me. The old black stud pulled his cock out until just the head was in, and immediately slammed it back in. The friction only letting him get about three quarters of his shaft into me.

"Agggh, fuck" I cried to entice Mark.

I drove my heels into the carpet, my legs trembling uncontrollably.

"Your cock is so fucking big, you black bastard!" I said.

"Fuck, you're just tight," Al said. "But we'll take care of that right now!"

The brute pushed harder to force more of his thick cock up my cunt while Mark watched.

"You just need a big nigger cock to come over here and service you!" he added.

Al was probably wondering how my cunt could tighten up so much since a year ago when Alvin and the gang bang boys thoroughly opened me up.

My legs continued to shake and tremble from my pussy being opened up. I cried out to intensify the experience.

"God your cock is so fucking huge," I cried, "I can't take any more!"

"Sure you can, baby," Al said as he pushed the cock further into me.

I started to moan uncontrollably from the feeling of having my cunt opened up by the humongous black cock. I felt so open and vulnerable, laying on my back as Al once again cracked open my cunt.

I didn't want Mark to realize that I was a size queen, though, so I was sure to let him know about the experience.

"Ahhhh fuck, Mark, I can feel his cock in my womb," I moaned out.

"Oh, God, Mark . . . he's just taking my tight cunt."

Mark was losing all sympathy for me at that point. In fact, it had a hint of anger.

"You fucking bitch! You said you could wanted a black cock! Now take it!"

By then Al was finally in to the root, his cock head firmly lodged deep into my spasming cunt. I could feel his heavy balls resting on my asshole.

Having heard the go ahead from Mark, Al brought his hands to my legs and lifted them high in the air.

"Let's see if we can loosen up the tight cunt of yours for your husband," he said.

As the great pounding began, I was barely able to see Mark as he stripped. Al pulled his long cock out of my cunt, rubbing the head against my cunt lips. He then slowly worked the snake back in until his balls rested on my ass again.

The black cocksman did this a few times, loosening up my cunt. He suddenly stopped that maneuver, instead slamming his cock deep into me with great force. The long dicking began, this huge baseball bat working through my cunt.

With each deep thrust, the sound of Al's heavy ball sac slapping against my ass echoed through the room. It was a decadent sight for Mark to behold, I'm sure.

Mark told me later that it was incredible seeing my legs spread so wide, the big black club stroking my fully stretched my cunt as I moaned uncontrollably.

Al added to the moment.

"So, baby, how does it feel to have a big black cock stroking between your legs?"

I was in heaven.

Here I was with my tits hanging out, my heels sticking straight up in the air, my skirt hiked to my waist, getting thoroughly laid by this big black bastard as my husband watched.

It was too much. Another orgasm ripped through me like a tidal wave.

"Fuck me, you fucking horny nigger," I groaned, "split my tight white cunt open with that black monster cock."

Al seized his opportunity.

"Mark, my man, your wife's gonna be a fucking slut for black cock by the time I get done with her!"

By then Mark was getting into it, having walked over to get a close up view of the fucking.

"I told you, Al," he replied, "she's a horny slut."

Marked paused for a moment, as though he finally realized what I had become.

"Yep, my wife's a fucking slut who loves big hard cocks."

Al was more than happy to prove him right.

"Then let's make her beg!" Al responded.

I moaned as Mark responded.

"I guess so," Mark said, "make her earn it."

Al jumped at the opportunity to make me earn it.

"You hear that, you pretty cunt, your old man wants to hear you beg for my cock," he told me.

The pounding intensified, the massive black cock stroking furiously through my cunt. My whorish moans weren't a good enough answer.

Al pulled his cock out completely and just rubbed the massive cock head against my clit. I pushed my hips up to the cock, whimpering as I silently begging him to put it back in.

"Well, wifey, how bad do you want my thick black prick, slut?"

I forced the words out as my body violently shook from the intense fucking.

"Ok, I'm begging . . . please slip that cock back into me Al."

"I don't know baby," Al responded. "If you really wanted it, you'd be begging a lot more than that!"

I was becoming lost in lust. As with every time in the past, I started to lose all sense of reality and what was around me.

"Oh, God, fuck me. Fuck me. Please. Give me that black cock you fucking nigger! JUST FUCK ME!" I screamed out.

“That’s it, baby, Al responded as he slipped the cock head back into my cunt, “here’s your big stiff nigger cock!”

By now Mark had his pants of and was jacking off watching he incredible spectacle as Al went on pounding me. It must have been quite a sight. Al didn’t even have his pants off. We were both fully clothed, Al’s pants down between his ankles and my dress hiked up.

Al added more vile remarks the whole time.

“Ahhh . . . Take my black . . . cock, you . . . white bitch,” he kept saying as he continued to pound me.

“Take my big black cock up your tight white married cunt!”

I was right with him.

“You fucking black bastard, tear my married cunt apart!”

“Stretch my tight pussy open with the big black prick!”

With that last comment, Mark brutally grabbed my tits as Al deep fucked me. It was as though he was going to punish me for being such a slut. God, how I wanted to be punished!

"How's that black cock satisfying your horny cunt, Andrea?" Al asked.

I moaned out loud.

"God . . . I . . . love it . . . ,"

I groaned louder as Al slammed me.

"Fuck, use my cunt to jerk off your big black cock!"

"I think you got a black cock slut here," Al said to my husband.

Mark didn't care, falling right into the moment.

"Fine, then we'll get my wife bigger black cocks," he said, "right slut?"

I was a horny wench who would do or say anything at that point.

"Oh God, you fucking . . . horny . . . black bastard," I responded, "I need a bigger cock!!!"

"We'll get you some real hung niggers to service that tight twat of yours, you fucking white bitch!" he responded.

Al had been pounding me for a good 30 minutes. His body was hot and sweaty. I couldn't believe what a master stud he was!

But Al couldn't last forever.

It wasn't long when I could feel Al's cock swell, ready to inject his black seed into my cunt. God, if my husband only knew that these big black balls had already emptied into me many times before!

"I'm . . . gonna . . . cum," Al moaned.

The memories came flooding back. I remembered how Al had been so intent on filling my womb with his bastard child, and then letting a pack of 50 horny black men inject their seed to increase the chance that they would impregnate me.

I thought for sure that Al was going to blow inside of me, but a sense of sharing apparently came over him.

"Mark, my man, I don't want to mess her cunt up too much before you get a piece . . . ," he said as he dismounted.

"So I'll just drop my load up here."

But he still wanted my cunt.

"I'll . . cum . . . in your wife's . . . tight . . . cunt . . . later!"

Al crawled up and straddled my chest, his big balls resting in my cleavage. He then jacked his cock furiously over my face until the first spurt came flying out.

"Ahhhh . . . I hope she likes cum!" he grunted as he doused me with his load.

I was surprised by how much cum Al had in him. He must have been storing it up since we met last year! He dumped an incredible load all over my lips and cheeks, huge thick globs pilling up.

I brought my hands to my mouth, and in an instant they were thoroughly covered. The massive webs of cum stuck between my fingers and ran to my chin.

I licked and lapped as much of it up as I could while Al stood up over me dropping every last ounce.

"Fuck, look at your bitch wife eat cum," he said to Mark.

Everybody was in heat.

"Go ahead Al, get right over her and dump it all on her," Mark encouraged him.

"Come give her some more!" Al encouraged him.

Mark was quick to agree with the suggestion. Kneeling up over my head, Mark pointed his cock to my face. It felt incredible as his cum started to drip down to my head. He was shooting his wad in no time, covering my forehead and eye lids. I sucked it all up like a hungry whore.

When it was all done, I laid there exhausted. Mark handed Al a beer and they both looked down at me.

Al was the first to talk.

“Your wife is a fine piece of ass, man, very fine indeed!”

“She is a great lay,” Mark responded to the Mandingo stud.

I was surprised when Al expressed his gratitude.

“You were an incredibly generous guy for sharing your wife with me, man!”

Mark returned the compliment.

“I appreciate the fact that you helped service her for me!” he responded, “she’s insatiable for big cocks!”

If Mark only knew just how true his statement was . . . but I think he was beginning to see that.

“Can’t keep a horny slut like that away from hard cock,” Al said to Mark.

“I don’t intend to,” Mark replied.

Al capitalized on Mark’s statement.

“She looks like she’s still horny. Why don’t we take her upstairs and get some more?” Al asked.

Again, Al didn't wait for an answer. He scooped me up in his big muscular arms and started for the stairs. Mark didn't object. He just sheepishly followed.

Al was heading for our bedroom. The black bastard was going to lay me in my marital bed!

Chapter 36

The cocksman carried me up the stairs to my bed as my husband followed, that massive black cock sticking out to lead the way. Mark followed intently, allowing another man to carry his beloved wife to bed her.

As we made our way to the bedroom, I brought my head close to Al's and whispered in his ear.

"Thanks Al, thanks so much!" I said.

He smiled with his approval.

As soon as we got to the bedroom, Al laid me down on the bed and started sucking on my tits. I held my black lover's head in my arms as he enjoyed me.

Mark looked at me and turned to go to the bathroom. As soon as Mark was gone, I had to ask Al for more help.

I knew my ass was going to be an issue. Al was an ass monster. I don't think he ever let a white woman go without taking his cock in her ass.

My mind went back in time. I remember how Bill and Al both ass raped me, helping to turn me into an anal addict.

And boy was I!!! I had every intention of having this black beast stroke off in my asshole tonight.

But how to do it?

Mark thought I was an anal virgin. I always yelled whenever he even accidently went near my ass. I couldn't just immediately love it!

I knew Al would find a way, so I asked him.

"Al, I really want you to fuck my ass," I told him. "But Mark thinks I'm an ass virgin who hates anal sex," I whimpered.

"Can you help me find a way to open him to that? Please?"

"No problem, sweetheart," he responded, "let me take care of it."

Al paused for a moment and grinned at me.

"You know 'ol Al ain't leaving this house without enjoying that fine tight ass of yours!"

I pulled him head up and had his lips inches from mine.

"Good," I said, and then gave him a deep loving kiss.

Mark came back as I was in Al's arms kissing him. I think it may have bothered him seeing me freely kissing a big black stranger like that – one who held me like a conquering stud with his prize. But I really believed in our marriage and knew it would be alright. I had to believe.

I gestured with my hand for Mark to come over to me. As he sat on the bed next to me, I turned my head away from Al and gave Mark the same kiss.

"I love you sweetheart," I whispered in his ear.

"I love you too," he responded, "so you go ahead and enjoy yourself tonight."

While I was kissing Mark, Al turned me on my side facing Mark. Al was behind me, raising my skirt so he could rub my ass.

"Damn woman! You have the whitest, softest, tightest little ass!" he said.

While Al stroked my ass cheeks, I pulled Mark to lay down in front of me. I pushed close to Mark's body, grinding my cunt into his pecker. Al pushed closer too, grinding his cock against my ass cheeks as he started to kiss my neck.

God, I was in heaven!

As Al licked my ear, I continued to kiss Mark. Al started to intensify the moment.

"Mark, my man, you're lucky to have a wife like this," he said. "A gorgeous, sweet fucking machine with a wicked tight pussy and big tits!"

Mark was noticeably proud.

"She's the greatest," he said, "she'd fuck an army if I asked her to."

I don't know if Mark realized what he just said. If he only knew that Al had arranged for a small army of black men to fuck the shit out of me last year!

As Mark kissed my still-sticky mouth after his last comment, I could sense that Al was thinking up a way to do it again.

"Mmmm, an army, I bet that would be quite a sight!" Al said.

The three of us laughed. We talked a little bit more, all nasty sexual comments about me and groups of black men of course.

As we talked I did what I did best. I administered to horny cock. Throughout the discussion I was stroking the cocks on my sides, squeezing them each the men said something I particularly liked.

As the guys talked some more about the vile things they would like to do to me, I bent down and took Mark's cock in my mouth. Al turned around and started kiss my ass checks, probing his fingers into my asshole. Every now and then he would slap my ass - hard!

I deep throated Mark for a few minutes before turning myself around on the bed. I then leaned in the other direction and crammed Al's slab of black cock meat as far down my throat as possible.

"Mmmm, you have a hell of a cock sucking slut here, Mark," Al said.

"Yeah, I love to get head as soon as she gets home from work," Mark responded.

"She looks great taking cock in her business suit, and then lapping a load from her face," he added.

"Man, I'd love to see that!" Al said.

He went on.

"And damn! How 'bout those loads she was taking down stairs!"

Mark smiled.

"You ever seen your wife take so much cum?" Al asked.

Mark was honest.

"Actually," he said, "I've never imagined a load like yours!"

"Well, my man," Al said, "I think this little bitch is most attractive with a massive load of cum on her face. Maybe we can work on that some time!"

Mark sensed that Al wanted to come back, but he obviously wasn't sure yet.

"Well, its up to her," he responded.

"If she wants to get creamed, I'll hold her while you jack off on her!"

Enough talk, I thought.

I thoroughly deep throated both of the horny fuckers. I was ready for more cock between my legs.

"Hey, is somebody gonna slip a prick up my cunt, or do I have to go a bar?" I asked.

Mark laughed, reminding Al that it was his turn. I was still on my side facing Mark. I waited with anticipation to see how he was going to mount me.

Al answered the question.

"Let me help you," Al offered as he hiked my skirt and lifted my leg for Mark.

Mark slipped right between my legs, his stiff prick in his hand. Al stayed behind me, grinding his cock into my ass as Mark mounted me, holding my leg up by the ankle the whole time.

"Man, I love this woman!" Mark said as he entered my well-fucked pussy.

"An absolutely gorgeous, horny vixen!" Al responded.

Mark was now all the way in me. He definitely noticed a difference.

"Fuck me, what the fuck did you do to her?" he said. "It's like fucking an oil barrel!"

Al understood.

"That's OK, my man, the lady'll tighten up again in a few days!" he comforted Mark.

Al was always a wise man. He added some reassurance to Mark.

"Your wife needs it, man, but we'll make sure you get the first piece next time!"

Ah, an open announcement that Al expected there to be a next time!

Mark shot back, apparently embracing the idea of another encounter with Al.

“Damn right,” he said, “sloppy seconds on my own wife doesn’t work when a horse cock is in the room!”

Both men started laughing as Mark started fucking me.

“Hey man,” Al said, “I didn’t blow in her yet! She’s that wet all on her own!”

My husband wanted to rectify the problem of my cumless pussy. He immediately started to long dick, slamming into me hard so he could get a little friction for his cock.

It was terribly wet for him, but Mark had an answer for his problem. After a few strokes, Mark pulled out his cock and grabbed the bed spread. He wiped off his cock and then roughly drove it back into my cunt.

“Ahhhh, that’s better!” he said as both men laughed again.

As Mark used my cunt to get his prick off, I reached behind me and grabbed Al’s throbbing prick.

“I want to suck your cock so bad, Al,” I whined.

Al pulled himself up until his groin was at my head. I turned my head up and sucked on the black cock. I was absolutely fascinated by Al’s magnificent cock, slowly stroking it lengthwise with my nails as I gently kissed the giant black cock head.

I soon felt a need to take the huge prick as Mark stroked my cunt. I sucked the black print into my mouth while giving the shaft a furious hand job. I then reached over and rubbed his giant balls.

“I want to take your balls,” I said.

Al re-positioned himself, dropping his big hairy ball sac into my mouth. I sucked on his big balls as Mark continued to screw me.

“Ahhhh,” Al remarked.

“A rare find. A bitch who loves to suck balls!”

The sight was too much for Mark. I could soon feel him stiffen, ready to blow his load into my cunt.

“Ohhhh . . . fuck,” he said.

“Blast your hot cum up my horny cunt!” I teased him.

Mark started to grunt and moan.

"God damn slut wife, here's some cum for your horny cunt!"

Mark then started to shake violently, and I could feel his throbbing cock jerking wads of cum into me. This had to be the most intense orgasm Mark ever had at any time during our marriage.

When Mark was done, he fell over on his back. Al piped in.

"How 'bout a turn for Al, his horny old cock would like another piece of that fine cunt."

Now it was me who didn't wait for an answer. I just crawled up to him, squatting over his massive shaft. I straddled his chest, taking his big cock in my hand.

I hiked my skirt up to my waist and guided the massive black head to my cunt. I freely impaled myself on the black pole.

"Ahhhh . . . Ohhhh . . . fuck," I said as I pushed more and more of it into me.

Damn, it was tight, but I just kept pushing myself down on it. I moaned the whole time, the feeling of pushing that massive cock into be being absolutely overwhelming.

"Ahhhh fuck, what a cock!"

I pushed it about half way in, holding myself up by placing my hands on Al's chest.

Al wasn't satisfied with my performance. The black stud brought his rough hands to my waist and gripped hard. He forced me down onto his cock the rest of the way.

"Ahhhh . . . Ahhhh . . . oh . . . fuck," I moaned as the cock stroked itself in.

"Use my cunt to get that horny prick off you horny black bastard!"

With that comment, Al lifted me by the ass and slammed me back down on his cock as hard as he could.

"I'll use that fucking cunt of yours," he said, "to jerk off my stiff prick."

Al proceeded to do just that.

He reached around and gripped my ass tightly. He repeatedly lifted me up and slammed me back down on his cock. You could hear Mark's cum being squished out of me by Al's massive cock.

Over and over, Al used my cunt to service his hot prick. He paused periodically to add his commentary.

"Now this is the way to jerk off!" Al proclaimed.

"Oh . . . fuck . . . what a tight . . . tight . . . cunt," he added.

When Al was almost done with that game, he reached up and cupped my tits. He rubbed them gently, telling Mark his options.

"You want me to blast my load with her on top of me?" he asked. "Or you want me to roll her over and pound it in?"

"How you want it baby," Mark asked me.

"I don't care!!!!" I cried out. "Just fill me with some seed!!!"

Al then grabbed my tits tighter, and used them to pull my face to his. As soon as I was close enough, he slipped his tongue into my sticky mouth.

He continued to kiss as he brought his hands back down to my waist. It was an incredible feeling getting slammed on his huge black cock while he kissed me, all in front of my adoring husband!

Al truly was a sharing man, there's no doubt about it. When we stopped kissing, he pushed me off from him.

"Your old man needs to get sucked," he said.

Ah, doggy style!

Pulling me off the bed, Al stood me up facing the bed. He got behind me and wrapped his arms around me. Mark positioned himself on the bed in front of me.

I could feel Al's massive, throbbing cock probing between my legs as he stood behind me, so I spread my legs to let his cock in. The great cock slipped in rather effortlessly, having opened me up so much on the bed.

As soon as Al was in to his balls, he put his hand on my back and pushed my face onto the bed between Mark's legs.

"Get your cock in her mouth, man," he said to Mark.

Mark was taken in by the show, but quickly snapped to the moment.

"Yeah, blow me," he told me.

I did as I was told. I took Mark's cock into my mouth and started to suck him hard again as I got fucked from behind.

Al's thrusts were intense, each stroke slamming me into Mark's cock. Mark put his hand behind my head to steady me, holding me onto his stiffening prick.

I sucked the stiff cock into my throat, moaning from the feeling of having two men take me at once. I was relishing every stroke into my cunt and mouth.

Al fucked me relentlessly for at least 5 minutes. By the end I could feel my legs begin to tremble and give out. I stopped sucking Mark for a moment to express my concern that my legs were getting tired.

Al handled the situation like a pro. The old stud pulled out of me and instantly gave me the simple command.

"On your knees wife."

I quickly complied, taking Mark back into my mouth as Al kneeled down behind me. He hiked my skirt and lifted my ass so he could slip his big cock back into me.

Al continued with his brutal fucking, doggy style on side of bed. He leaned over to whisper a question in my ear.

"You like taking two cocks at once, baby?"

My mouth was stuffed with Mark's stiffening prick, so I gave an affirmative moan and nod of my head.

"How's that blowjob," he went on to ask Mark, "She getting you hard again?"

Mark moaned that he was hard again, to which Al came back with a reply.

"Good, cause we're gonna help your little wife really take two men at once!"

I don't think Mark understood what he meant, or if he even heard him given the ecstasy he was feeling from my deep throat blowjob. I knew what Al meant.

Chapter 37

As far as Mark was concerned, my ass had never known cock. What would he do when this black bastard moved to crack it open?

Al started his move.

"Your wife's gotta nice ass," he said to Mark.

He then leaned over and loudly asked in my ear.

"You take it up the ass, baby?"

Mark immediately perked up. I was afraid that he might try to intercede on my behalf, not wanting me to get hurt.

I stopped sucking and raised my hands to Mark's chest. I looked him right in the eye, finding a way to remind him of our deal.

"We're gonna let this stranger do whatever he wants to me?" I asked Mark.

Mark was speechless.

"Oh God, Mark, this black stud's going to take me up the ass with that fucking huge prick of his. What do I do?" I insincerely asked.

"Andrea, I don't know. I don't want you to get hurt. What do you want?"

"I want you to be happy," I said, "and you always wanted to ass fuck me. Maybe I need to do this for you."

"It's up to you," he said.

I was there!

I looked back and locked eyes with Al. I asked him politely.

"Al, would you please fuck my ass?" I cooed. "My husband really wants to see me take it in the ass!"

Al was right on it. The black bastard wasted no time. He immediately took control and gave the instructions.

"Get on your knees and lift that ass for me," he commanded.

I pulled myself up, resting my elbows on the bed. Al grabbed my waist and yanked me up until my butt was sticking out for him. He told Mark to grab a pillow and put it under my head.

As soon as the pillow was in place, Al ruthlessly pushed my face into the pillow.

"Mark, you hold her down. Your bitch is going to scream at first!" he said.

Al started to work his fingers into my asshole, spitting down on my sphincter muscle to lube it. He then told me what he was going to do to me.

"Ok, baby, here 'ya go," he said. "You want some hard cock? I'm gonna crack open that tight little virgin ass of yours with a big black cock!!!!"

With that he quickly plunged his cock up my cunt doggie style. I gasped at the unexpected sensation. I guess he was trying to lube his snake from my dripping cunt.

The black stud stroked my pussy a few times, slapping his big ball sac against my cunt lips. He then withdrew his cock and split my ass cheeks with his powerful hands.

Al started rubbing the massive black battering ram through my crack, searching for the pink little hole he was intent on destroying. My anus twitched in anticipation of the anal drilling that was about to come.

"You better take it easy on her, Al," Mark interjected. "She's gotta real small ass . . . ," he added.

Al cut him off.

"Don't worry, Mark," he said, "I guarantee your wife will be an ass slut by the time I'm done."

"She'll beg you to fuck her ass every night!" he promised.

That perked Mark up. It was the one thing he always wanted me to do, but I always flatly refused. With a promise like that, how could he refuse Al my ass?

Al finally found the mark and pushed the cock head against my anus.

I had to give Mark a good show. I couldn't let him know that I was already an ass slut! An ass fuck is always an experience, no question about that. As the huge cockhead popped my ass, my mouth flew open and I screamed out.

"Agggggggh . . ."

Al didn't stop.

He grabbed my waist and pushed a few inches of his cock in.

"Agggggggh, . . . f . . . u . . . c . . . k," I slowly groaned.

Al continued the assault on my ass.

My head went straight up in the air, and I cried out again.

"It's ok, baby," he said reassuringly, "we're almost there."

The fucking liar! I'd be surprised if he had 3 inches in me. He had 11 more inches of stiff black prick to go!!!

Al pushed more of his cock up my ass, further tearing it open. I had to give a good show for Mark, so he'd truly believe I was an ass virgin.

"Oh fuck, please stop, Al," I cried, "you're fucking tearing me apart!"

That did it for Mark. He tried moved to get Al to stop, but Al just pushed him back.

"PLEASE! You goddamned fucking nigger, you're killing me!" I screamed.

Al didn't stop. He kept jamming the fat cock into my asshole. He was about half way in by now.

"Oh god, please, you're splitting me in two," I cried, "your black cock is just too much."

Al shot back as Mark held me down even tighter.

"Fuck you, Andrea, you and your old man told me to open your ass, so I'm opening it!"

"Ain't no turning back now!" he boasted.

I looked in my husband's eyes and gave him a whimper.

"God, fuck . . . I did . . . ask for it . . . didn't I?" I slowly groaned out.

Mark just shook his head in disbelief.

"Fuck . . . Mark . . . that . . . big . . . cock is . . . making . . . my ass bleed!!!"

Al was silent as I cried. He just grabbed my ass cheeks and pushed harder.

"Agggggg . . . Aghhhhhhh," I cried over and over as more and more of the massive black cock literally ass raped me in front of my husband.

Mark looked down as Al suddenly pulled his cock out of my ass. He then swiftly jammed it straight up my pussy again. Needed more lube, I guess. In an instant he was back at my ass.

The old stud pushed harder and harder, more of the thick shaft driving into my bowels. Probably 9 inches by now, I thought. At least 5 more inches for my husband to see rammed into me!!!

I was crying out, my head sticking up in the air, uncontrollably moaning for mercy as Al continued to talk to us as he brutally rammed me.

"Fuck, man, Andrea's white ass sure is tight," he said coldly.

He apparently didn't remember that Mark had never enjoyed my ass.

"You really need to ream out your beautiful wife's ass more often."

Al pushed again, and he was close. The coke-can thick cock had me wide open. He pushed again, and then I felt his balls on my cunt.

"OK, bitch, it's in. I'm just gonna let it rest there for a minute while you suck your old man."

Mark turned his body. I dutifully lifted my head and took Mark's cock in my hand. It was rock hard and sticking straight up. I held onto it as a way to balance myself against the intense ass fucking that was sure to come. But I was getting hotter. I took it in my mouth, licking up and down his shaft as the lust started to work over my body.

Al held his hard cock in my ass for a good minute while my asshole adjusted. He added more commentary while he rested.

“Ah bitch,” he moaned, “feel every inch of my throbbing black cock in your bleeding tight ass!”

I could feel it. I could feel every vein of the monster cock as it throbbed deep in my guts. I tried to relax. I knew Al wanted to give Mark a real show. I was going to get a real ass reaming by the black fuck monster. I grabbed on to Mark’s stiff prick to steady myself.

Al suddenly pulled his cock all the way out of me without warning. My asshole snapped shut as soon as the giant cock head was dislodged.

As with the last ass fucking Al gave me, he immediately jammed his thick cock back into my ass, but it was too tight again to get all the way in. He thrust hard into me again, cracking me open again. You could actually hear his heavy black balls violently whack against my cunt.

Al did this over and over, totally ripping my tight asshole ring wide open.

I cried out each time, as if on cue.

“Oh God please! It hurts Al!” I cried, “stop . . . raping . . . my ass!”

Mark tried again to stop Al, pulling his prick out of my hand. But all I did was enrage Al, sealing my fate that so he was going to ruthlessly ass rape me.

"Stay away man!, or it'll really hurt her," Al said.

Mark came back up to me and put his arms around me. He rubbed my head as the black brute towered over my ass.

"It'll be ok honey, it'll be ok," he reassured me as he kissed my head.

Al deeply pushed his coke-can cock into my ass over and over. After a few minutes of this, he pulled out and started to stroke me slowly. After a few strokes, me pushed it all the way in again.

"Oh God! Oh God! Please no!" I pleaded.

Al slowly stroked the massive cock through me again and again.

"Don't worry baby, you're almost an ass slut!" he boasted, "rub your clit!"

I knew rubbing my clit during as ass fuck always got the emotions and lust to a frenzy point. So I did as I was told. I reached down between my legs and started rubbing myself through my slick hairy bush. The harder he fucked, the harder I squeezed my clit and pulled on my sticky cunt lips.

I was paranoid.

I knew I was going to lose myself to the lust very soon. I felt Mark needed more. He needed more of a virginal protest before I snapped in lust.

"Oh God please, it hurts!" I cried.

"Please . . . Aghhhhhh . . . please," I whimpered.

"Rub your cunt harder you stupid bitch!" Al growled back.

Al continued to slow stroke my ass, hitting rock bottom again and again. I felt his balls resting on my cunt lips. Then he would stroke some more.

Faster, and faster, and faster.

Harder, and harder, and harder.

The black stud was building a rhythm.

In response, I fingered myself as deep and hard as I could, rubbing the hairy black ball sac every time it slapped against my cunt lips.

"Now I'm gonna really crack your virgin white ass open!" Al proclaimed.

My husband watched as the Mandingo stud started to deep stroke my ass faster and harder. He was buzz-sawing his cock through my anus. Vile comments flew from his mouth.

"Man, this horny bitch wife of yours sure needed a good ass fucking!" he said.

Al stroked off his cock in my ass more and more, pulling it out and slamming it back in. The great cock would come all the way out, and then get slammed in to his balls. Out and in. Out and in. Harder. Faster.

"You needed a big black nigger cock stuck in your hot white ass, you horny cunt!" Al grunted.

I guess begging is always in vogue. I knew I had to show Mark that Al broke me, like a new horse.

I started moaning. As Al humped my ass harder, I moaned louder. Harder and louder. Harder and louder.

Al knew what I was doing, and he played along like a pro.

"Oh, fuck, you like it now, don't you bitch?" he deeply moaned.

I moaned my approval.

"You like a big cock up your virgin ass, don't you Andrea?" he asked again.

I moaned louder in approval.

“You like your ‘ol man seeing you with a big black cock up your tight ass, don’t you?”

“Ugggh . . . Ahhhh . . . .”, I groaned in approval.

“Oh fuck man,” Al said to Mark.

“Now your wife’s got a great big black dick stuck up her ass!”

Mark started to laugh as I gave in to the lust. He could see that Al was right, that it wasn’t all that bad after all.

By this time, I was panting like a dog in heat. My head began to swoon and thrash, my hair flying around my head. Thick strings of drool escaped from my gaping mouth each time Al’s massive cock head rolled through my guts.

It was finally time to send the signal to Mark that I loved this feeling of being ass drilled. I looked back Al and let him know it, too.

“Ahhhh . . . fuck,” I moaned.

“Ahhh . . . damn it!”

“You . . . black . . . bastard!”

“My . . . ass . . . Ughhhh!”

"Yes, . . . fuck . . . my . . . ass!"

"Work . . . your . . . big . . . prick off . . . in my ass!"

That was all Al needed to hear.

"Then get back to blowin' your ol' man, and I'll give you some more black dick in your ass!" he said coldly.

Mark then got back in position, opening his legs so I could rest my head on his prick.

The old stud then gripped my ass with one of his hands and immediately began long dicking my asshole with such force that my face was again being slammed onto Mark's prick.

Being driven mad with lust, I looked at Mark and told him what I wanted.

"Fuck my mouth like a cunt, you dirty bastard."

I took Mark's shaft and shoved it down my throat. I was grateful when he grabbed me by the ears and started working my throat up and down his cock.

Each time Al drove his cock home, I impaled my throat on Mark's stiff prick. I was now totally limp, having fallen into my natural place in life. I was being used as a fuck hole by two incredibly horny men. No energy was required.

Al's force-fucking of my ass pushed my head onto Mark's cock with each stroke, each withdrawal pulled by body backwards because my ass was so tightly clutched on the invader. All I had to do was moan like a whore satisfying her studs.

Ah, my two beautiful studs!

The men were also at a fever pitch. Al yelled out as he drilled my ass.

"Moan for my big black cock stroking your asshole, you fucking horny white bitch!"

Mark was right behind him.

"Swallow my cock while this black bastard drills your ass!"

I pulled Mark out of my throat to yell out a response.

"Now I'm a fucking ass whore, make me moan with your hard cocks up my ass and down my throat!"

Now Al wanted to enjoy my pussy too. I thought it was kind of gross when he did it before, but it was incredibly exciting. No man had ever done this except Al.

Al would pull his cock out of my ass, and then get immediately jammed straight up my cunt until his balls hit. Next stroke -- out of my cunt and jammed up my ass until his balls hit. Next stroke, next stroke, cunt, ass, cunt, ass.

Harder and harder.

I felt like my face was going to go through the roof as the buck nigger jerked his cock off in both my ass and cunt.

What a feeling!

I was in heaven from the sinful ass banging, but Al was now ready to up the ante. The old bastard withdrew from my ass and wrenched my face off from Mark's cock. He wrapped his arms around me and brutally grabbed by two tits.

In one swift move, Al swung me around and lifted me off the bed. He spun me around to show Mark my gapping asshole, lifting my skirt to reveal the damage he caused.

"How's that for an ass reaming, ever think you'd see your pretty wife's asshole look like that!" he howled.

I could tell Mark was amazed, but that he loved it. In retrospect, it must have been a hard experience for Mark.

Helplessly watching this big buck nigger, an old stud with a massive black cock, his firm ass and muscular body towering over me, as he savagely raped his pretty young wife's "virgin" ass before his very eyes!

"Oh fuck!" Mark exclaimed.

"I can't believe it! I can't believe Andrea is loving it in her ass!"

Al was quick to respond as always.

"Her fucking asshole can look like that every night!" Al said.

"Can't it Andrea?" he turned to me and asked, "you'd like that every night, wouldn't you?"

"Oh . . . God . . . fuck yes!" I responded enthusiastically.

With that Al withdrew his cock from my ass and pushed me over on my side so my ass was facing Mark. Always a gentleman, he was inviting my husband to enjoy what he cracked open. It was kind of like offering the crab meat to the poor bastard who couldn't crack open the legs!

This would be the first time Mark would experience double penetration. In fact, I think it was his first time at anal sex. I wanted to make it a wonderful experience and memory for him.

The black stud moved around in front of me and laid down. Spooning me, he lifted my skirt and pushed my top leg to the side. He started to expertly work his big cock back into my cunt.

"Ahhh," he said, "I'd love to open her asshole every night!"

I moaned my whorish approval.

"But it's your turn man!" he said, "she's your wife!"

Al took a few strokes in my cunt as Mark intently watched us. He then looked at Mark and invited him in again.

"Come on Mark, come lay behind your wife and slip your cock up her ass while I fuck her cunt!"

Mark was obviously unsure of his skills, but he clearly loved the idea. I was rooting for him.

"Oh God sweetheart," I groaned, "I want to feel you in my ass while this black bastard is taking my cunt!"

Mark got behind me and did exactly as he was told. Al buried his cock into my cunt and reached behind me. His muscular hands spread my ass cheeks wide for my husband. My asshole was still gaped, waiting for him to enjoy me.

“Slip right in here, my man!” he instructed.

Mark brought his cock in between my spread cheeks, guiding his throbbing cock into my gaped hole. His cock slipped right in. This was his first double fuck and his first true piece of ASS!

“Ohhhh fuck,” he said as he slipped into my gaping asshole, “I can feel your cock inside her!”

“Go ahead and stroke her man,” Al said, “she’ll love you forever!”

Mark started to stroke my ass, slowly at first and then with a growing intensity. My husband’s head fell backwards and he started moaning louder and deeper than I’ve ever heard him. I knew Mark was in sexual heaven.

The feeling of this double fucking also overtook me. A skillful DP has always been the most incredible, enjoyable sexual act for me. It drove me literally crazy with unquenchable lust.

“Give it to me guys,” I groaned. “God, I feel like such a whore. Ream me with those hard cocks until I scream.”

The men obliged, adding comments of their own.

"Ahhhh," Mark said, "I never thought I'd appreciate black cock like this!!!"

Al added to the comment.

"You're fucking wife is quite a fuck whore man . . . This bitch lives to service hard cock!"

The statements were all true. I moaned like a whore in approval.

"God, I love that big black cock of yours," I moaned to Al. "And I love your hot prick in my ass," I told Mark.

"Oh fuck, let me service your stiff pricks! Slam me harder!" I screamed.

By now Al had fucked me for an incredibly long time. Al was a true stud, no question about that. But even studs wear down over time.

Al grabbed my waist tightly. His thick cock worked in and out of my cock, his balls slapping against me. Then he started to slow down, making sure he could feel every stroke of my cunt walls. I could feel his body start to tense up. He started moaning, and Mark egged him on.

"Blow it in, Al. Flood my wife's steamy cunt."

Al appreciated it.

"Yeah, man, don't mind if I do!" he groaned.

"Ah, fuck," he moaned, "here's some nigger seed for your tight cunt Andrea!"

The thick black cock swelled in my pussy and then let lose a flood of hot cum into my womb. Al moaned like an uncontrollable madman the whole time, enjoying the feeling of blasting my reamed-out cunt with his black seed while my husband watched and encouraged him.

The whole time Mark continued to pump my ass, commenting that he could feel Al's cock throb as it blasted the wad of cum up my twat.

"Fuck, Andrea," Mark moaned, "you're so fucking hot! God I love you!"

When Al was clearly finished, Mark pulled out his cock. Reaching for my waist, he then pulled my cunt off from Al's softening prick. Mark rolled me onto my belly, pushing my face going into the pillow like Al had done earlier so he could take my ass like Al did.

"I'm gonna try to really fuck your ass Andrea," he announced.

"Go for it," Al responded, "I think she likes it better up the ass!"

I moaned with the comment as Al offered his expert guidance to my husband.

"Just spread those cheeks with your hands!"

I clutched the pillow under my head and moaned again.

"God . . . yes Mark . . . really give it to me!" I encouraged him.

Mark worked on slipping his cock into my asshole. Mark then got on top of me as Al had done. The black cocksman just laid next to us, sweaty and exhausted.

Al encouraged Mark the whole time.

"That's it man, hold those cheeks open and slip your dick in," he instructed, "she's pretty much broken in for you now."

Mark spread my ass cheeks as he was told, making it easy for him to slip his cock into my reamed-out ass. He easily pushed it deep in my bowels again, moaning with the sensation of the new hole.

"Agggghhh . . ." I moaned to him.

My ass was lose and wet from the brutal fucking Al inflicted on it, but Mark loved it nonetheless. He brought his arms up around my head and started whispering in my ear as he took my ass.

"You loved his big black cock up your ass, didn't you Andrea?"

I moaned loudly.

"You wanna feel big black cock up your ass all the time now, don't you?"

I moaned another loud affirmative response.

"You wanna take a big black cock up your ass and cunt at the same time?"

I couldn't believe my ears. Even in my lustful state, I was quick to agree.

"Oh god, yes! I want to be double fucked by hard black cock."

Al was loving the show. Mark was clearly a man after his own heart. All he needed was a little training, and Al was the perfect mentor.

"Goddamn, you fucking slut Andrea!" Mark cried out as he humped my ass.

He stroked me faster and faster, his lust overpowering him.

"You're my wife and you'll take any hard cock up your ass that I tell you to, right?"

I liked where the topic was going. I responded best I could as I was ass fucked.

"Oh God . . . yes!" I cried out.

"I'm your slut baby! Give . . . me . . . cock . . . I'll . . . service it . . . for you!!!"

Mark pumped harder and faster as Al enjoyed the show and conversation.

"Damn, I loved seeing you service our hard cocks," Mark groaned.

"I'm your fucking . . . slut . . . . wife, and . . . and . . . I'll fuck any cock . . . you tell me to."

Mark reamed my ass more as Al laughed at what was happening.

"Any cock," he said, "as many cocks as I tell you?"

"Oh . . . God . . . please Mark," I begged him, "please find . . . me cock, as many . . . as you want. I just . . . need . . . I need . . . hard cocks."

That was all Mark could take. In an instant his cum was blasting up my chute. My ass fell down, and Mark collapsed on my back.

The three of us all rolled over and quickly fell asleep. Mark was behind me with his arms around me. Al was in front of me, and I was wrapped in his arms. I was in heaven.

Chapter 38

The three of us slept in a heap all night, exhausted by all of the intensive fucking. And I still had some of my clothes on!

I heard Al get up and go to the bathroom during the night, and he came back and slipped his cock into me. We were both half asleep as he jerked his big cock off between my legs.

We all woke up about 9:00 in the morning. Al wasn't done with me. The old stud was ready to comment as Mark woke up and regained his composure.

"What a wife, man, do you know how lucky you are to have this fine a woman?"

Oh, Mark knew.

"I love this woman more than anything in the world, and if she wants cock, I'm gonna get her some big hard cocks!"

"Mmmm . . . ," Al went on.

"I sure wanna be your friend!"

With that I leaned over and kissed Mark, looking into his eyes.

"Can we be friends with Al, sweetheart?" I whispered in his ear.

"You are our friend," Mark said to Al.

Al was quick to accept the new friendship.

"I'm glad I could help . . . you seem like nice . . ."

I cut Al off by giving him a deep french kiss.

Me and my studs took turns going to the bathroom and cleaning up while the others laid collapsed in the bed. When the boys were finished, I got up off the bed and stood before the two studs who just took me.

I cupped my tits, and then slowly pulled off my open blouse, letting it fall to the floor. I then reached behind and undid my skirt. I slowly pulled one leg out of it, and then the other. I crawled on the bed between my two lovers.

"Your beautiful wife is going to be quite a fuck queen, Mark," Al remarked.

My husband liked the compliment.

"She is already," he boasted, "and I love her so much for it!"

"You guys have any kids?" Al asked.

"Two daughters," I responded.

I knew that surprised Al, because I only had one daughter the first time he seduced me. I could tell that he was wondering if one was black, but he probably remembered when I told him last night that I had never been with a black man. Thankfully, Al didn't let on to Mark that he was surprised.

"Nice family," Al responded.

"You want more, sweetheart?" Mark asked me.

"Kids?" I asked.

"No, sex!" he responded.

"Kids will come!" he joked.

Well, I'm sore," I said, "but I like seeing my studs get off."

"Try not to knock me up!" I joked.

"Yeah, right," Al said with a grin.

Mark then asked Al if he wanted to stay the day. I was happy to hear Mark ask Al. That meant he truly liked him.

"Our daughters are with their grandparents this weekend," Mark said, "so we can stud her all day long if you two are up to it."

I was quite surprised, but delighted.

Al readily accepted the opportunity to bed me non-stop for a whole day.

“Man, what a guy. I’d stud this hot wife of yours every night if I could!”

“I’m game,” I responded, “I love seeing you two getting off!”

I slid off the bed and lifted my foot. I reached down and slowly unstrapped my heels and slipped them off. Repeating the performance for the other shoe, Al and Mark made comments that I loved to hear.

“I told you I’d turn her into an ass slut,” Al remarked. “And man, turns out she’s a horny cum slut to boot,” he added.

“God, the ass of hers felt so great,” Mark responded with a huge smile.

I looked at them and spoke in a wry manner.

“I guess I’m just an all-around slut!”

Now buck naked, I went to the bathroom to freshen up. I made sure I grabbed my red lipstick and perfume as I walked back into the bedroom. I never miss an opportunity to excite a few studs, and lipstick and perfume for some reason gets a stud as hard as a rock.

As I slowly worked on the lipstick, I slowly licked my lips. Al had the best comment I heard yet.

"Lipstick must enhance the cocksucking experience!"

"I always wondered why she loves lipstick so much," Mark added.

I confirmed their suspicions.

"If you guys only knew how much lipstick makes me want to suck off a hard cock and eat cum!"

Al loved it.

"Buy this lady more lipstick!" he cried out to my laughing husband.

I jumped onto the bed, working my way under the cover between the two men. They took their cue and crawled in beside me. What a day this was going to be!

I got in bed and asked my studs if they wanted me to try out my lipstick on their cocks before they studded me again.

Mark didn't want just a blowjob, though. He threw back the covers and pushed me to the black man who was now openly sleeping with us in our marital bed.

"Al, hug my wife for a minute if you would."

Al was pleased with his new involvement in our marriage.

"I'd be happy to," he said, wrapping his arms around me.

I looked up at Al and gave him a long french kiss, only to feel Mark's hands splitting my ass cheeks. The fucker wanted another piece of his new found joy! I couldn't blame him, if it felt as good for him as it did for me.

"Ah, there you go dude," Al said to him, "practice makes perfect!"

"You better practice every day, you fucker," I sluttishly whispered to Mark.

My ass had tightened a little during the night, causing Mark to moan as he parted my asshole with his rigid prick. He then stroked me on my side, pushing me into Al's chest. Al and I deeply kissed as Mark took my ass.

"Fuck, I love your ass, Andrea," my husband said.

Al always had a response. He stopped kissing me to offer it to us.

"Yes sir, your pretty wife has an ass that was made to be regularly butt fucked by hard cock!"

I looked back at Mark and told him how much I wanted it.

"Ahhh, God . . . I love it . . .fuck my horny ass all day then!"

With that Mark pushed me more on my stomach, pressing my cunt lips against Al's leg. He started to long stroke me as I jerked Al's stiffening cock. Al was soon hard again, looking for more action.

"I think I'll stud your wife's cunt while you're reaming her ass!" he announced.

"Ah fuck yes," I moaned, "double fuck me again!"

Mark pulled out to allow me to mount our black stud. I whorishly moaned when Al pulled me onto his chest, guiding his big black prick into my quivering cunt.

Mark moved with my body, ready to stick his dick deep in my ass. As I pushed myself down on Al's huge cock, Mark was right on top of me, refusing to let anything stop the double fucking.

Al then used his strong hand to work my hips, pushing his long snake in and out of me as Mark thoroughly reamed my ass.

I participated in the double fucking with reckless abandon. My used, sore holes readily accepted their invading cocks. I started moaning uncontrollably from the double penetration, my swooning head thrashing around.

Al was quick to point out the obvious.

"Man, this wife of your is one cock-starved lady."

I let out a whorish moan as he continued.

"I bet she'd die if you don't keep hard cock jammed up her ass and cunt!"

"God, I wish I had a cock in my mouth too!" I responded.

Mark continued pumping away on my ass, slowing to answer the call.

"My little wife doesn't realize it yet, but after last night she's gonna have more cock than she knows what to do with!"

God, I sure hoped so!

I knew my love for Mark would deepen to an unexplainable level if he kept that promise! Here we were, finally after all this time. This man, my sweet husband, turned out to be a lascivious sex maniac like the other men I had fucked.

"I'll take any cock, all cocks, just give me a hard cock," I cried out.

Al loved it, pulling me down to kiss me. He then shared some of his feelings.

"You're a wonderful woman, Andrea, I love being in your bed with you and your husband."

I was being driven mad with lust.

"Oh god, stud me right here in my husband's bed with that big black cock while he watches you take me!" I cried.

Both men groaned when they heard my invitation.

"Fuck me deep and hard with that fucking black cock!" I cried as I tried to slam my willing body back and forth between my lovers.

It took some practice for me too. I worked on jamming my ass into Mark and my cunt into him in an alternating rhythm. From the increased grunts, I could tell I was doing a good job.

I was surprised at how long Mark was lasting. This new-found sexual release seemed to be the answer for his issues too! But I knew Mark was getting ready to blow his wad in my ass.

A few second later I felt Mark tense up. He wildly grabbed my tits to pull himself as deep into my ass as he possibly could, causing me to slam back against him as another orgasm ripped through me.

"Ohhhhh . . . fuck . . . Andrea," he cried as the first jet started to unload in my ass.

"I love cumming in your tight ass!" he exclaimed.

As soon as Mark pulled his spent prick out of me, Al rolled me over. His cock never missed a beat. In a flash the black stud was on top of me, my legs wrapped around his back. He wrapped his hand around my hand, slipping his fingers through my hair. He passionately kissed me as he slow humped me for the first time in our stormy relationship.

Kissing me as he truly made love to me drove me insane! What a feeling, I thought. A big black stud making love to me in my husband's bed while my husband watched, relaxing from the savage ass fucking he just gave me as my black lover's cock was lodged deep in my cunt!

Al worked his big cock in and out of my cunt as Mark got up to get cleaned up. Once Mark was gone, Al slowed his stroking of his cock, whispering sweet nothings in my ear.

"How'd I do, sweetheart?" he asked, "Can I come back?"

I wrapped my arms around his back and held him tightly as my cunt slowly met his thrusts.

"I think you're in for good," I whispered in his ear as I ran my tongue around the lobes. "As long as keep our secrets!"

"Oh baby," he moaned, "I'd kill men to keep your secrets safe!"

Al continued to slow stroke my cunt with his long black dick, holding me tightly around the top of my head. He talked to me more, whispering in my ear.

"God, I just want to fuck you and watch you get fucked," Al said.

I whispered back as I reached down to rub Al's beautiful, firm black ass.

"I think Mark will let you fuck me all you want," I said. "And maybe some of your friends too."

Al was clearly pleased by what I was saying.

"Don't worry baby," he said as he held me tight and started to shoot, "I'll . . . take . . . care of you . . . and your husband."

The Mandingo stud shot his wad between my legs with a deep moan, emptying his balls into me yet again.

Mark made his way back to the bed while Al was shooting, and he could clearly see that he was emptying his load.

"Pounding another load into my wife, huh Al?"

As Al grunted and moaned, he dropped his reply.

"Your little lady deserves a little nigger spunk up her tight little married twat!"

Mark agreed, matching Al's words.

"She can have all the nigger spunk she wants," he promised.

Once Al was spent and rolled off of me, Mark climbed onto the bed next to us. He held me tight while I rested my head on Al's muscular chest.

I laid there thinking about the wonderful night and day that developed, my lust problems finally resolved once and for all. As the men continued to talk about me, I drifted off to sleep again thinking about my incredible luck of finding such a wonderful husband – and a wonderful black stud as well!

My prayers had been answered!

I was pleasantly surprised throughout that day, both of my lovers regularly getting horny and sporting a hard-on as they slept. Each time they would just roll me over to use my cunt to stroke themselves off, instinctively slipping their hot pricks deep between my legs while half asleep.

We wasted the whole day away in bed like that, with me as their willing cum bucket. I must have gotten laid 30 times between last night and today!

Studs.

True studs.

Chapter 39

I woke up that evening to the sight of my two men smiling down at me as they stroked my tits. I must admit that I was one woman with two sore holes!

I smiled back and let them both give me a kiss. While they kissed me, I reached over and started rubbing their cocks. While he gently rubbed my tits, Al began to speak.

"This little wife of yours sure can handle black cock!"

My proud husband was quick to reply.

"After seeing what you did to her, I think it's safe to say my wife can handle any cock!"

I looked up at the men and licked my lips to confirm the truth of Mark's statement. I then brought my mouth down to their waists as they continued to talk, alternating a slow blowjob between the two men.

"That's right," Al started, "She did say she would fuck as many cocks as you told her to, didn't she?"

Mark remembered the line of talk.

“She’s going to be surprised when I take her up on that!” Mark said as he looked down at me.

By now I was deep throating the two cocks, bobbing from one shaft to the other, the whole time moaning from the thought of more hard cock.

Al couldn’t resist the opportunity.

“You think she could handle a foot and a half of hard black cock?”

Alvin the Impaler!

My mind raced to the experience with Alvin! Mark, not knowing that I already had, defended me as I moaned my approval.

“After what I saw last night, I think she could handle a fucking horse!” Mark said.

“Seriously, dude, my friend has a jet black, rock hard cock that’s every bit of a foot and a half. And it’s a big around as your arm! You really wanna see him destroy your wife’s cunt and ass?” Al cautioned him.

Mark paused for a moment and thought.

"You think you could handle that honey?" he asked me.

I paused for a moment. Alvin was pretty damn big. Ah, why not!

"I think I probably could," I said, not letting him know Alvin already enjoyed me once.

"Is he safe?" Mark asked.

I was very happy to hear the great concern my husband had for me. I was ashamed to realize that I hadn't been so cautious with my own health.

"He's safe. He's a good dude. No diseases, nothing weird. Just solid black cock."

Marked paused for a moment.

"Well, ok," he said softly. "We're in it this far, and I want her to be happy."

"You sure you want to try a black cock like that, baby?" Al then asked me.

"I'll handle that guy fine as long as you guys are with me," I responded.

"Well, then," Al continued, "I'll give Alvin a call and set it up. Just the four of us."

Oh my God! Three studs! My fantasy!

Mark thought about the idea some more and started laughing.

"A foot and a half? Hmmm, that would be quite a sight!" he said.

"A foot and a half, my man," Al said.

Al didn't want to lose the moment.

"Maybe next weekend?" he quickly added.

"Well, why not," said Mark.

Wow. Did Mark really know what he was saying?

I looked up at my studs and gave them my reply.

"Mmmm, I can't wait," I said, "you two can watch that big buck nigger crack my ass open!"

The men laughed, reveling in my whorish demeanor, laying back to savor their intense blowjobs. I hadn't stop slobbering on their luscious cocks the whole time.

Mark must have gotten excited by the thought of a huge black man using my body to jerk his monster rod off, because he soon started to erupt in my mouth. I never knew my husband to produce so much cum in such a short period of time!

I was surprised with the next comment Mark made while he shot his load in my throat.

"Shit, Al . . . maybe a gang bang . . . Yeah, a gang bang with a bunch of your friends!"

Al started laughing.

"You really want to see a pack of horny nigger studs take your beautiful white wife?" he asked with a grin.

"Well, it's just a thought," Mark replied.

I don't think Mark realized exactly what he was saying. But I knew if anyone could make it happen, it was my Mandingo stud Al.

Al knew what he was doing.

One step at a time is the sign of a true master.

"Maybe, Mark, but let's see how she does next weekend with Alvin first!" Al replied to Mark.

As I moved over to bob my head on Al's great cock, I started to get a little worried from the line of conversation.

A gangbang!

Oh my God, I wanted to try a gangbang again!!!

But how could Al possibly keep all those men from revealing our secret?

It was a problem for another day.

As I started to drink the hot load of thick cum that Al started flowing into my mouth, I realized that I was a lucky woman and that someone was definitely watching over me.

I looked up at the two studs who enjoyed me throughout the day, a giant wad of cum smeared all over my mouth and lips.

Running my tongue out to lap it up, I gave my response.

"I'll leave it up to my two lovers," I said. "You just tell me where to be guys, and I'll make sure nobody goes home disappointed!"

The men pulled me up, both of them holding a part of me. We all laid in bed laughing, fully immersed in the realization that I would forever be their beautiful, willing fuck whore.

It turned out that getting ruined by Bill and used by Al were the best things that ever happened for my marriage!

Chapter 40

I am so happy things worked out for me and Mark. I truly love the man and my family. I didn't ever want to lose that, but the sexual awakening I experienced left me in a terrible quagmire. But I prayed every day, and the good Lord eventually found a solution for me.

I am truly happy for Mark. He has never asked me if he could have another woman join us, so I've never had to deal with the jealously that would obviously bring. No, my husband is happy just seeing other men bed me. So I have kept my promise. No man beds me unless Mark knows about it and agrees.

Wow, the road I traveled. It turns out that the life I lived were his fantasies the whole time. Through a strange twist of fate they are now a reality for him. And it was due in no small measure to Al.

That black motherfucker ended up being best friends with Mark! Hell, Mark and I even backed my lover financially when his bitch ex-wife took him to court for more child support. And Al sure didn't let us down with Alvin! He was a man of his word, and my secrets have been safe.

As for me, I have my husband and my regular lovers - my Mandingo studs - Al and Alvin. I haven't fucked or sucked Jack since that day he pissed me off. Jamar calls the bank for me at times, but I stay away from him too. Yes, I am addicted to cock. But Mark has given me what I need to keep it in check. I couldn't be happier.

Mark and I also discussed this whole issue of HIV and stuff, and that was the clincher. We decided we would pretty much stick with these guys. Sometimes we even invite Nickie over, although he is still a little young. (But I did confirm – he is over 18!) But I still love fucking him!

Now, my black studs come over regularly to service me, I'd say at least three times a week. Sometimes Mark and I watch porn with them, which usually ends up in some kind of fuckfest. I have to tell you, I could give Kayden Kross and Jane Darling a run for their money!

As for the gangbang, yes, it did happen. It wasn't easy finding people who didn't know my secret, who could keep the secret of my whoring ways, and who were safe. So we ended up with Al, Alvin, Nickie, Joe, Travis and, of course, my husband. Six cocks! What a weekend! But that's a story for another day.

Well, Jennifer, so ends my story of my path to becoming a happily married nymphomaniac. Yes, believe it or not, Mark and I continue to go to church every Sunday. I do not have a moral problem with my new lifestyle, nor does Mark. We are good people and we treat people right. I think that is all that God wants. Most of all, I think God wants us to be happy. For the first time in my life, I am truly happy. Mark, too.

Perhaps this change I endured and came to enjoy was destiny. Or perhaps divine intervention. I don't know. All I do know is that it saved my marriage and kept my family together. I can now sleep peacefully at night, and every day is a wonderful new adventure.

I hope your readers find the same peace that I found.

THE END

Author's Perspective

Shaved pussies.

I have a refrigerator magnet with a cartoon image on it. It shows a woman standing in front of a sink with a razor in her hand. The sink has a small animal in it with shaving cream all over its furry face. Of course, the animal is a beaver. The caption reads, "Sometimes husbands have the strangest requests!"

Do they really?

I have to say, I have a extremely thick, bushy pussy. My husband goes crazy over it. Why, then, do most women in modern porn have shaved pussies? Explain that to me. Please, someone, explain that to me!!!

Personally, I think it's disgusting. Yes, a number of my female friends shave their pussies. Ok, they seem to like it. But men? Most – if not all – of the men I've discussed this with say that they HATE a shaved pussy.

Well, I won't tell the adult industry what to do. They make a lot of money, so maybe they know a group of men I don't know. Personally, I think they're wrong.

As for myself, I'm keeping the fur that God gave to me. My husband loves it, and I do too. Quite frankly, it just isn't real sex unless their's a bone going in a thick, bushy cunt! That's my opinion, at least. And that's why every wife in every book I ever write will have a massive, furry bush!

As for the porn industry, whatever floats your boat folks. BUT, if any producer ever has a prayer of getting the rights to turn one of my books into an adult film, I can guarantee you that hairy pussies will be an absolute requirement. Don't forget that!!!

– Jennifer

www.ingramcontent.com/pod-product-compliance
Lightning Source LLC
Chambersburg PA
CBHW021010180626
46814CB00003B/1227
9780983522522